# OOPS!

# OOPS!

Chloe Richards

The Book Guild Ltd
Sussex, England

First published in Great Britain in 2005 by
The Book Guild Ltd
25 High Street
Lewes, East Sussex
BN7 2LU

Typesetting in Baskerville by
SetSystems Ltd, Saffron Walden, Essex

Printed in Great Britain by
CPI Bath

A catalogue record for this book is
available from the British Library

ISBN 1 85776 834 5

*For the people who showed me the light during those dark months: my family, especially my beautiful and infinitely patient mother. For Catherine, Robert and James who opened their home, their hearts and my future. And of course, thanks to Naked Man.*

# INTRODUCTION

It is three minutes past midnight on New Year's Day and a new year is finally here; it stretches before me like a blank tapestry, waiting for the threads of my life to merge and overlap until they create an undefined, unbreakable confusion of colour and shape; but this year it will be different.

This year the threads will be neatly trimmed and the colours will harmonise, until at last the pattern emerges. What the final image will be I have no control over, but it will be clear and precise and it will be mine.

I am not running away – not any more.


It seems that the New Year is a time for promises and change; tears of regret wash out the old year, as declarations of love ring in the new. Promises are made as hearts are broken and we each have a regret of our own.

Time does not heal; time allows us to grieve and to live with what has happened, but it does not and should not heal; how can we learn from past mistakes or past regrets if all we have to do is wait for time to cure our ills? They will and should stay with us forever and hopefully that way time will not reconcile; it will teach, and what it teaches us will be beyond learning and beyond regret. Time allows us to live, to make mistakes and to survive some of the choices we make. It tutors us and shows us that despite support and love, despite loneliness and despair, we are accountable only to ourselves and no one else can carry us through this life.

A bad mistake is a bad mistake and it can perpetuate or it can die.

The choice is ours.


When I began these diaries I had no idea that they would accompany me on the long arduous journey that finds me where I am today: they were meant to be nothing more than frivolous unimportant entries made by an over-excited bride-to-be with nothing more to occupy her mind than frilly dresses, colour schemes and ridiculously priced cakes.

Looking back, it is easy to see that they were my salvation; my way of coping in a world that was becoming increasingly lonely and increasingly desperate. On rereading each of the earlier entries, it is clear that I *should* have seen the signs; they were, as they always are, there.

In fact I think I did see them. I think both Greg – my future husband – and I both saw the signs and we both chose to ignore them. So when you hear people spout the predictable mantra, 'The warning signs are there', try to resist the urge to smack them, because they're not lying. However, what these people fail to mention is that when you're in love – or when you *think* you're in love – and when you trust the person you're with, you don't really *look* for signs – why would you? And if you're not looking for signs, how the hell are you supposed to see them?

It's only afterwards, when things begin to fall into place, that you think 'Oh yeah, crikey, I think that might have been a sign' and you give yourself a mental headslap for being so dumb.

A lot has changed over the past few years, but the biggest change has been in me. It was a barely perceptible change, more of a lethargic transformation that took years to complete; no one noticed, not even me. I stopped being open, loving, honest and confident. I became cold, distant and aloof, I lost my confidence and locked myself away in a world of make-believe, I over-compensated for my lack of confidence by being vibrant and 'vivacious', but inside I was dying to retreat to the only place I felt safe: home.

It sounds ridiculous now, but it was as though a veil had been drawn across me; I was still there, I could still see and be seen, but there was no clarity, no substance. I perpetuated the myth that I could cope with anything, and that I could cope on my own; I didn't need anyone. I think it's safe to say that this was my defence mechanism – if you don't rely on someone then they can't let you down.


My life has been thrown into turmoil, I have been to hell and back, and I have no one to blame but myself. I had the chance of a new life and I blew it. I made mistakes, which were followed by more mistakes, which were followed by even more, until I finally couldn't cope, but I wouldn't admit it; on the surface I was happy and carefree, but inside I was dying, slowly, day by day, and I stopped caring, and started waiting.

I was waiting for the pain to end. I was drowning beneath a rising tide of emotion and I couldn't swim against it. There was no way out, it was consuming and hateful and finally I stopped fighting and went with the flow.


These diaries were meant to be my way of explaining things to myself, of trying to work through my decisions. They were supposed to help me *understand* why I did what I did, why I am the way I am, and hopefully to help me forgive myself for being the person I have become.

*

3

In reality they have made me laugh and they have made me cry, and finally I do understand. I just hope my mother understands when she discovers that her daughter has slept with men for money; though it was lots of money, Mummy, and they were all rather posh and I did fly in a helicopter and you can bet your arse that Martha Pepplin-Stewart's daughter wouldn't be paid so highly for *her* services so that's one up on her – see! I told you I'd do you proud!

I have been a bit of an arse; I allowed myself to be manipulated, to be changed and then I made a balls-up of the new life I had a chance of. I pushed people away, but I've stopped pushing now. Chloe is on her way back.

When I was finally able to reread my diaries, only one word popped into my head: *oops!*

What more can you say when your less than perfect engagement becomes a warning beacon that forebodes a tempestuous marriage which in turn has the life-span of a gnat, and the fallout of both sees you clinging helplessly to the rocks as the tsunami that is your life abates and life in a new world is washed up at your feet.

Oh, and you have sex with rich men for no less than £2000 per night (including lunch, dinner and/or cocktails and the occasional flight in a helicopter).

I began my diary the day after the 'proposal'. It was to document my life as a bride-to-be and thereafter, as a newly-wed. It was supposed to chronicle the ups and downs of organising a marriage: the tears, the laughter, the ups, the downs, until finally the euphoric event that is a marriage came to pass.

In fairytale-bride-land, I imagined that I would keep it for years and pass it down through generation after generation until my name became nothing more than a hushed whisper of awe and inspiration; a name synonymous with perfect, true and everlasting love.

Arse!

Didn't quite go to plan, but it began well.

If only I'd read the signs.

Because do you know what?

They were there . . .

## 30 April 2001

*16.30-ish.* (Time is irrelevant now – who needs time – I have forever!)
Oh hurrah, hurrah, HURRAH!!!
The impossible has happened.
The question has finally been popped.
After six years, four months and five days I have been proposed to.
Happy, happy, happy!!!

*16.35-ish*
Actually, it was not so much a proposal, more of an 'are we going to get married then or what?' And yes it did come after I began to pack my bags and leave him, because he said he would never ever get married, but the outcome will be the same so who am I to split hairs? *I* am getting married. Not at this exact moment (sadly) but one day.
Sooooon-ish.

*16.37-ish*
He didn't even get down on one knee.
And there's no ring.
Not exactly how I planned it, but hey ho! Am getting married!

*16.40-ish*

Have called mum at work to tell her the good news.

Couldn't understand a word of what she was saying, she was too busy crying. Not sure why she was crying. Thought she liked Greg.

Will assume that it was mum-speak for 'I didn't think you'd ever find anyone who would put up with you'.

Think she is happy.

She has always assumed that I am far too challenging and headstrong and independent, and anything else that means I have a mind and a will of my own. I just know what I want that's all. And I like to get what I want.

Or at least try.

*17.03-ish*

Tis lovely here on cloud nine, very snug and cosy. Trying not to walk around with a coat-hanger sized grin on my face. It is impossible. My cheeks are beginning to ache.

Greg is very quiet. I asked him if he was okay. He said yes. Then I asked him if he was sure he wanted to do this. Didn't really want to hear his answer but thought it polite to ask. Fortunately he said of course, he was just thinking about when the date for the wedding should be.

Crikey. He really does mean it.

This time round.

*17.30-ish*

Will not think about the other time we were engaged.

There wasn't a proposal that time either. We were just walking past a jewellery shop and he asked me what I thought. Told him I needed the loo, and thought it strange that he was asking me what I was thinking, I didn't think boys did that.

He said, 'No, what do you think of the rings and do you want to get married?'

Didn't know what to say, we had only been together for ten months. Thought it was a bit soon but there was a sparkly thing involved, and I did love him so I said yes, and I meant it.

Greg on the other hand didn't. He buggered off after just a few months of engagement. He changed his mind and left: no warning signs, nothing.

I got home from work one day and whoosh! No Greg; just an empty house and an echo where his voice would have once been. Houdini couldn't have done better. Except I don't think Houdini left notes behind saying 'Sorry, I just don't think I can. I love you.'

He came back after six weeks and asked if we could 'talk', and after wrestling the kitchen knife out of my hand we sat down and did the talking thing, and several hours later he admitted that he had felt trapped and that he had proposed too soon – hmm, thought I'd already bought that one up – and could we try again?

But am not going to think about that.


*18.10-ish*

Will also not think about the time he threw the same engagement ring over the garden fence and told me that he would never ever marry a woman like me and he didn't know why he had come back, he must have been mad, who the hell could put up with someone as selfish as me anyway, I was far too opinionated blah, blah, blah.

Never did find the ring – ah well, didn't like it anyway.

I imagine a twenty-third-century Tony Robinson will dig it up and study it for months before announcing rather capriciously that it is an indication of the idiotic romantic gestures of a bygone age.

And how right he would be. In fact there would be nothing capricious about that, except he will never know that the

8

ring was thrown away in a nasty millennium eve drunken argument by a nasty control freak.

So nope, I'm not thinking about that.

Am thinking instead of pretty dresses and parties and being the centre of attention.

And being married.

And feeling wanted and being secure and loved.

And belonging.

Hurrah!

Will not worry about nasty things, will get bucket of sand and bury my head in it.

*18.45-ish*

Have called our friends Jayne and Andy, who are newly-weds themselves and will be forever indebted to me – I introduced them a few years ago and they are now happily married – *I am* an angel sent from heaven to do good upon this earth.

*18.52-ish*

Jayne and Andy have turned up on the doorstep, Jayne armed with bin liner full of wedding brochures, Andy armed with a look of compassion and a 'are you really prepared for the long, drawn out months ahead of you' look for Greg. They also have two bottles of champagne. They are most welcome!

*19.25-ish*

Had a Chinese meal and lots of champagne. Jayne was saying something about stress and arranging weddings. Didn't really listen to her.

How can a wedding be stressful?

*21.00-ish*

Am horribly full. Feel a bit sick. Thank God I don't have work tomorrow.

Can't face going into work when I'm on such a high, and anyway I want another bottle of champagne. Jayne and I have been talking 'weddings'. I am now a fully-fledged member of the 'wedding' gang. I can now take part in '. . . and did this happen to you?' and '. . . oh well, when *I* was organising my wedding . . .' conversations. Eugh – those conversations have always bored the arse off me. That and computers and *Star Trek*, and *Star Wars* and role playing games.

Greg likes all of the above, with the exception of wedding conversations of course.

I'd rather boil my head in a vat of acid than sit round a table wearing a pointy hat having a deep and meaningful conversation about how the Games Master is God and his word is final, sounds very *Lord of the Flies* if you ask me. 'I'm the Games Master, I've got the conch, I'm the best. I am God!'

Anyone who's anyone knows that God is a pair of beautiful shoes that not only look good but are also very comfortable. Therefore God is Enzo Angiolini.

*22.06-ish*
Andy and Greg have disappeared. So long as Greg reappears for the wedding and I still get to wear 'the frock' and be gushed over I don't really mind.

*22.18-ish*
Am I missing the point of a wedding?

*22.20-ish*
No, of course not – It's all about looking pretty and being the centre of attention, is it not?

Jayne has asked where and when we plan to get married. Tell her it will be in Italy next summer. Hurrah!

*22.22*
Now all I have to do is tell Greg where the wedding is. And when. Will tell him when I find him.

*23.00*
Found him. Was wearing pointy hat in study and discussing something called cyber punk.
Seized the moment and during a brief pause in his conversation told him we were getting married in Italy. He said, 'Yeah, okay, whatever you want.'
Whatever I want. Hmm.

*23.06*
Hurrah!


**1 May**

*09.56*
Eugh! Whose head is this? When did a parrot crawl into my mouth and do its business in there without my noticing? Who is the strange yet handsome George Clooney come David Boreanaz-like man lying next to me? What are these rose tinted glasses I appear to be wearing?

Aha! That man is Greg. My beloved. My intended. My husband-to-be.
Eugh! Not sure I like the sound of 'husband'. Eugh! Like the sound of 'wife' even less, strips one of one's identity. Never mind. Will get used to it I'm sure.

*10.37*
Double eugh! Am *not* having his surname. No way. Uh-uh. NO! Think it best that I keep that to myself. I'm sure it

won't come up in conversation. We'll discuss it after the wedding, but I'm not changing my mind! His name sucks.

*19.17*
Greg has decided that he would like his brother Leon to be his best man. Leon, as it happens, manages a bar in the city centre – I feel another celebration coming on.
Oh hurrah!

*00.45*
OH MY GOD! Went to bar. Had champagne. And cocktails. Fell asleep in the toilet.
A thousand Roman soldiers are stomping through my brain *en route* to my stomach, where they will no doubt set up an overnight camp and then resume their stomping in the morning. I have to be up at 6.15.

*00.57*
Feel sick.

*01.00*
Am going to be sick.

*01.17*
Was sick.


**2 May**

*06.58*
Soldiers in full stomp. Think they have set up a look-out in my brain; this will tell the main camp the precise moment I have to talk to someone, at which point the main camp will

then empty out their overnight slop trays, the smell of which will emit from my mouth.

Do not feel very attractive.

*07.07*

Have looked in the mirror. Am not very attractive. Face is grey. Lips are swollen and outlined in a dry white substance. Think it may be dried vomit. Gorgeous!

Need liquids. Lots and lots of liquids.

Eugh!

Have to sit on train emitting horrid stench whilst surrounded by po-faced business men.

Arrghh!

Also have to accompany the library director to a rather swanky author affair. And I smell like a raccoon.

Pants!

*12.43*

Have to go out at lunchtime and pick some brochures for 'Weddings in Italy' or similar. Am supposed to be updating the library website with a list of forthcoming events.

Am not. Am looking at wedding dresses. Am naughty.

*12.51*

I'm off to get the brochures, oh how wonderful!

Have done precisely two minutes of work today. Which is more than usual.

Getting married is so productive.

*13.30*

Oh my God that hurt!

The sun was blinding, and I had to shy away from it. Think I may have been bitten by a vampire in the night. Wasted trip. No brochures out yet, with the exception of one.

Pants.

Too tired to look at it. Will look at it later. Much, much later, when the alcohol in my body has been replaced with blood.

Has the illusion of marriage left me so soon?

*13.40.*
Uh-oh! Forgot about the swanky author affair! The library director is heading straight for me! Does not look happy.
Uh-oh!

*14.03*
Phew! Am so lucky. Library Director came to tell me that the swanky author affair had been cancelled. Showed correct amount of disappointment.
He then told me that I looked ill and should I really be at work? Milked it and said I'd be okay but if I felt worse I'd go home.
So.
Library director now thinks I'm an angel. Hurrah!
Except now I have to do horrible research.

*15.25*
Should be working not writing in my diary.
Don't care.
Anyway, am supposed to be doing research on the internet and this looks like I'm taking notes. Have decided to take a sneaky look on internet at the prices of getting married in Italy. Tis naughty, but this is important! Besides I don't think it matters what Birmingham's poet laureate is doing in five months' time. Writing poetry. Probably.
So I'll just pop that in my notes.
Hmm.
Have looked at the cost of getting married in Italy. Begin to cry. Will concentrate on poet laureate instead.

## 5 May

*11.00*
Greg's birthday today.
He's managed to book time off work in order to celebrate.
Bless the West Midlands Police and their thoughtfulness,
they are most kind. Hmm. Whenever I want him to book
time off it seems they can't manage without him. Most
strange. Almost as though he hasn't actually asked them for
the time off.
Hmm. Almost as though he doesn't *want* the time off.
Will not think about it.
There's a party this evening. Jayne and I, however, have
more immediate plans. We're off 'frock' hunting. Visit a
shop on the high street that always has amazing dresses in
the window. I am determined not to spend a huge amount
of money on a dress that will only be worn once. I can't
think of anything more silly.
Disgusting and wasteful to do such a thing.

*14.17*
Am knackered.
Have already tried on oodles of dresses and feel like a
princess. All of the dresses are very, very reasonable. Hurrah
for me and my money-saving ways!
Knew I could do it.
Think it helps that I know what I want: I do *not* want
anything sparkly or too fancy. Eugh!
Am not going to look like a loo-roll holder.
The women in the shop were very good at stuffing me into
the dresses and knew exactly what style suits me. However,
at one point they held up a disgusting dress that had lots of
awful crystals sewn into it. It was hideous. Horrid. Refused
to try it on. Am now having lunch with Jayne and she is

15

trying to talk me into trying the dress on: 'You've got nothing to lose just by trying it on have you?' she says.
Suppose not.
She also asked what I was going to do 'with all that hair'. Cheek! What does that mean? Have head full of dark unruly curls that's all. Sometimes look like Kate Bush that's all. Greg fancies Kate Bush. Used to say I looked like her. Hasn't said it for a while. Hair straightening serum is a good thing: stops one from looking like a horny, slightly off kilter pop star.
Hmm.
Perhaps I should throw the serum away? Told Jayne I didn't know what I was going to do with 'all my hair'. She asked me if I'd be getting it cut. Asked her what she was trying to say.
Bloody cheek!
She then said I have lovely hair and she hoped that I wouldn't be getting it cut short because in 'that' dress I'd look like a movie star. Ahh.
Love Jayne, she's lovely.
And she always tells the truth.

*15.00*
Want that dress! Not shockingly awful at all. Tis a dress made by the Gods in heaven and is only fit for a princess, AKA *me*. I have a size eight waist, and size 36dd breasts – at least in this dress I do.
Want it.
Tell the woman in the shop that I want it. She tells me how much it is. Cry.
Then sulk.
Not fair.
Want it.
Stupid, stupid dress. Stupid, stupid assistants.

*03.47*
Back from the party.
Greg's sister is visiting from Canada and has brought her gorgeous 20-month-old daughter Grace with her. Everyone at the party is absolutely smitten with Grace – she is the centre of attention. Toyed with the idea of asking if Grace can be bridesmaid. Then I noticed how absolutely gorgeous she is, how she is the centre of attention and how absolutely smitten everyone is with her.
Decide against it. Perhaps I don't need a bridesmaid after all. Will only detract attention away from myself. Nope. Don't need a cute little bridesmaid.

*04.13*
Am a bit worried about a conversation I had with Greg's mum. We were discussing whether or not I would change my surname.
Didn't think it was an issue.
Of course I'm not.
Greg overheard the conversation and said, 'Of course you *are*' in a voice that challenged a response.
Oh dear. Methinks there may be trouble in paradise. Best not to think about it. I'm sure he'll have forgotten the whole conversation by tomorrow.

## 6 May

Shit!
Conversation not forgotten. Greg insists that I take his surname. Don't want his surname. Want my own. His surname is cack.
Am sulking.

*11.30*
Tried to compromise and suggested that I have a double-barrelled name (though it does sound a bit silly). Absolutely, one hundred percent-idly NO.

That's that then.
For now.
I am *not* having his surname. But for quiet life will pretend I am.
Am sneaky.

*17.00*
We had to go into the city centre to pick the car up, stopping off on the way at a sidewalk café. (It all sounds so New-York these days). It was actually a vastly overpriced high street coffee chain that had tables and chairs outside – but that doesn't sound as 'chic'.
The coffee is overrated, and overpriced, but I'm a sucker for a gimmick and hand over my money with the willingness of a child.
Popped into a few travel agents – still no brochures. Or at least, no brochures with wedding packages in with a price that I am willing to pay. Why is that when the word 'wedding' appears in front of a product or service the price increases by 50 per cent? Were I a cynical person I would think that all these companies were trying to 'cash in'. But I'm sure that would never happen. Perhaps I'll try the internet again, cut out the middleman.

**12 May**

*13.40*
Have bought the very expensive wedding dress.
Uh-oh! Don't care. Wanted it. I'm paying for it so why

shouldn't I have it? Am very happy. Will look like a princess. Just need a wedding now. Not getting very far on that front. Never mind, I'm sure it will be easy peasy once the ball gets rolling.


**19th May**

Quick recap of the week.
Mon: Work. Home. Look on internet for advice on getting married in Italy. Bed.
Tue: Work. Home. Look on internet for websites that arrange weddings in Italy. Bed.
Wed: Work. Home. Look on internet for the best of the websites that I have previously looked at and ask them for quotes (think it is a very ominous sign that the prices have been omitted on the websites). Bed.
Thurs: Work. Home. Check email to see if any of the aforementioned companies have been in touch. They have not. First rumblings of panic set in. Is this an impossible task? Bed. Nightmare about getting married in a submarine.
Fri: Work. Home. Check email for quotes from the internet companies. I am sure they will have replied by now. They have not.
Sulk.
Drink.
Drunk.
Bed.
And that was the week that was.

It is now 12.45pm on Saturday.
I am still in my nightdress (which is actually one of Greg's T-shirts – must take it off before he comes home and sees me in it – think he might be wearing it later).

19

I have not had a wash/shower/bath or indeed a quick splash.

My early morning breath is now much enhanced by the aroma of stale coffee.

I have gone blind.

The internet is a source of much information. It allows one to book holidays, to arrange insurance and it will even organise a wedding in Italy for you. Or at least give you the names of the companies who will organise the wedding.

These companies offer a wide range of services. All you have to do is contact them with your query. This is where the said companies are very, very, very bad. They do not get back to you. On that they are very, very, very bad (I had to mention this twice, because it deserves to be mentioned twice. They are bad. Very bad at returning email queries).

I have a friend at work whose family is Italian. She has told me not to worry, and it's just the Italian way. Apparently they never hurry things. They will get back to me when they get back to me. Think that when they get back to me it will be bloody obvious that they have got back to me, by the very fact that they have got back to me. Do not say this to her because I'm just in a bad mood.

Want this wedding sorted.

Still at least we have over a year.

We have decided on a date.

It will be on *Friday 1 June 2002*.


## 17.00

Hurrah for Italian people. They rock! Oh joy and bliss. Not only will I look like a princess but I will be getting married in a fairytale princess castle.

Have been swanning around with bits of toilet paper tied around my head and hanging down my back and humming the wedding march (which I'm not actually having), trying to get myself all princessyfied and regal.

Lucky, lucky me.

Not only that but Greg has said that I can be in charge of *everything*, so long as we keep to the agreed budget.

How very, very kind he is.

I am the luckiest girl alive.

He has said that he doesn't care where we go, what we do, or how we do it. I can arrange it all and decide on all of it. *Bliss*! I get to do everything!

The email from Italy was from a very, very nice woman called Rebekah. She is a Canadian based in Italy and will arrange and coordinate everything for the wedding. She suggested the castle in Italy followed by a reception in the grounds, with torches and candles and lots and lots of wine. We (I) want a very simple but memorable day. Nothing too fancy (with the exception of the big fairytale castle), and nothing formal or stuffy. No speeches etc. The company Rebekah works for will obviously charge an arrangement fee, but they will deal with all of the Italian paperwork and arrange a translator etc. It is still a better bargain than the 'package weddings' you find in the holiday brochures. And we can have a three-week honeymoon.

Oh, even more joy and bliss!

I get to arrange that as well!

Have the luck of the gods shining down upon me.

Life is perfect and will remain so forever.

## 9 June

Who the freak does the Queen think she is?

Have had to change the date of the wedding!

Apparently its Queenie's Golden Jubilee or something on the weekend of 1 June, and the following Monday will be a Bank Holiday. If this is true, then you can bet that travel over that weekend will be very expensive. Also, Jayne is not sure if she can get that date off work.

Decided to change the date to 5 July instead; that way we will be on our honeymoon for my birthday!

Have told Rebekah, she said that this should be fine, as the castle has not confirmed our booking yet. She will tell them that the date has changed and as soon as they have confirmed she will let me know.

Happy.

Happy.

Happy . . . ish.

## 14 June

No news.

Getting worried.

Lord only knows what Greg does with his time. Never see him. If he's not working he's doing something else. Perhaps we should spend more time together.

Must not let wedding consume all of my time and it most certainly should not be the only thing I talk about. Will find Greg and spend quality time with him.

*19.17*

Shit.

Can't find him.

Mobile switched off.

Not at friends.

He didn't mention working overtime.

But then if something has happened at work he'll have no choice but to stay behind. Tis the peril of being a policeman. Tis pants being the future spouse of a policeman; you never know where the fug they are. If they're not working oodles of overtime, they're in the pub 'bonding' with their shift.

Seems Greg is rather fond of bonding. So long as it involves alcohol and the word 'wedding' isn't mentioned.
Git.


*20.40*
Where the buggery fuck is he? I have no social life, spend my time either at work or tied to the goddamn computer trying to arrange his wedding and he does a sodding runner.
Selfish git.


*21.19*
Have had argument with selfish git.
Came home at nine and told me in a blasé manner that he had been for a drink.
Would not elaborate, would not talk, just buggered off again to 'get away' from me.
Wanker.
Only wanted to spend some time with him.
Have smashed very nice crystal glass. Was aiming at his head. Missed head and hit the wall. Now have smashed glass to clear up and have damaged the wall and am crying. Hate this non-life I have. Wish I hadn't agreed to get married. Arranging weddings is pants. *Weddings* are pants. Bet marriage is pants as well.
Hate Greg.
Am cancelling the wedding.


## 15 June

*09.18*
Am not cancelling wedding. Have made friends with Greg. Made friends at just gone one o'clock this morning when he

23

finally came home. Am not going to ponder on his whereabouts.

*11.00*
Think the wedding company has gone bust.
Super. Re-secure myself a husband only to have the wedding company dissolve.
Super duper.


## 16 June

*10.54*
Have a reason to leave the house today! Hurrah! It's Jayne's birthday and we're all off for a meal. I'm not driving so I can get a bit squiffy. Hurrah! Will *not* sit in front of the computer waiting for emails. I am not a slave to that computer, I am an independent woman with a will of her own.

*11.03*
Will just check email before I go out.

*00.04*
Met Jayne and Andy and Nick and Amanda in the restaurant. Had lots of wine. Also had a teeny bit of food. Nick and Amanda had to leave early. Never mind, all the more for me! Someone had the bright idea of going back to Jayne and Andy's, which I also thought was a very good idea at the time as they always have oodles of alcohol. Jayne decided that it would be a very good idea if we all played 'Pictionary'. I have issues with Pictionary. No one *ever* wants to be my partner in Pictionary. I am the fat girl in the netball line-up

24

that no one ever wants to choose for their team when it comes to Pictionary.

Hate the bloody game.

Played Pictionary. Jayne was very kind and agreed to be partner. Had to draw 'popcorn'. Easy-peasy. She thought it was a penis. In all my Pictionary playing days have never picked a card asking me to draw a sodding penis. Was clearly popcorn. Then had to draw 'poison' so I drew a skull and crossbones.

She thought it was one of those ice-creams shaped as a foot with a face on it.

Used to love those.

We don't win.

I sulk.

We then play 'Articulate' and I convince Jayne that I'm fantastic at this game.

Am super articulate library type person after all.

She agrees to be my partner. We lose.

*1.03*
Depressed.
No news.
Drunk.
Sulking.


## 18 June

Why is life so cruel? Still sulking. Not very constructive but it makes me feel slightly better to bring other people down with me. I'm not a very nice person today. Can't remember the last time I woke up and didn't immediately think 'wedding' thoughts. My life is no longer my own.

Also think I might be getting premature age lines. Have been pulling all sorts of faces in the mirror and each one results in an array of lines. Will never pull those faces in real life anyway so perhaps I shouldn't worry. Asked Greg if he thought I had lines. Said 'no don't be silly'. Without even looking at me!

Git.

Then asked him what colour my eyes were and shut them tightly so he couldn't see – am adult. Assumed this was a very safe question, we have been together for almost eight years after all. Of course he'd know.

Hmm.

Waited patiently for his response. After a while he still hadn't answered so I peeked through slitted eyes at him.

He'd gone!

Felt a mixture of anger and fear – why fear? And went off to look for him.

He was in the kitchen making a drink and smiled a cheeky smile at me.

Ahh. Do cheeky. I laughed at him and asked him again what colour my eyes were.

'Swamp green,' he said.

Hmm.

Never has anyone described my eyes as swamps before.

They are not like a swamp! Have lovely eyes! Mother told me so. They're green. Or hazel. Depends on what time of year it is. Not sodding 'swamp!' Bless Greg and his romantic ways.

Git.


**19 June**

*10.12*
Hurrah! Dolce vita! Finally had an email about the wedding!

*10.17*
Pants. Dolce crap-a! Have actually read the email. It appears the castle has had a query from a large company about hiring it on 5 July 2002!! The castle has obviously given priority to the said company because they can offer more money. Try to obtain the number of the castle in order to call the 'big boss man' person and tell him that there is more to life than money, and does he not know that he is ruining my – oops! – *our* – big day?!? The castle is not listed – which is to say I didn't actually try, but it sounded good in my head. I just accept the cruel reality of this world like the big brave soldier I am. And then sulk.


## 20 June

Another email from Rebekah.
Semi-good news.
The castle haven't actually accepted the booking of the big bad company – it was just a provisional booking and the company have until Saturday to confirm. So all I have to do is wait until Saturday . . . easy.
Ho-hum.


## 22 June

Checked email.
Nothing.
Tum te tum.

## 23 June

Was up at the crack of dawn – that's to say ten – which is the crack of dawn in Saturday language. Lots of coffee. It is now 3pm. Nothing. Scared to go anywhere in case an urgent email comes in and I have to give an immediate answer. Am prisoner in my own study.

*12.13*
Need the toilet.

*12.16*
No I don't.

*12.19*
I do. I really, really do.

*15.32*
Think I have given myself a urine infection.

*16.06*
Nothing. Really have to pee. Have I got the day right? Shit. Hope I shouldn't be at work.

*16.34*
Nope.
It's Saturday.

*17.00*
Give up.
Watch paint dry and kettle boil.
Finally go to the toilet.
Convince myself that green urine is perfectly okay.

*02.15*
Looking on the internet for other places to get married in. Sulking. Think I used to live with someone. Never mind – can always grab another man off the street and marry him.


## 24 June

*12.03*
Nothing. It *is* Sunday though. I don't suppose they work on a Sunday. Have looked on the internet and found another venue offered by Rebekah's company.
It is still in Tuscany but this time in a villa, and not only can the guests stay in the villa but both the wedding and the reception can be held there as well.
Cheer up a bit.
Still don't know where Greg is. Think I might have put him under the patio.


## 26 June

*17.18*
Nothing. I knew it. They've gone bust! Either that or it was a pretend website and they were only after my money!! I've been had! Duped!

*18.00*
Greg has just pointed out that we haven't actually handed over any money, so we haven't been robbed. Hurrah!
That just leaves the bankruptcy option then. They've gone bust. Selfish gits.
How dare they?! Don't they know who I am?

*18.13*
Greg has just said that 'No they don't know who you are and they wouldn't care anyway, not if they've gone bust.' Told him to get lost.
Where did he come from anyway? Haven't seen him for ages, and suddenly he's there dishing out good advice and other crap. Oh why was I put upon this earth to endure so much frustration?

## 27 June

Have to remember that I am very lucky. There are lots of people worse off than me. Still, they don't have to organise the impossible do they? Have heard nothing.
Nothing.
Nothing.
Nothing.
**NOTHING!!!!!!**

## 28 June

'I feel pretty. Oh so pretty. Oh so pretty and witty and gay!!'
Have had an email at last. The company have decided *not* to book the castle, so we *can* have it. YIPPEE! I *will* be Cinderella! I *shall* go to the ball. Send Rebekah an email to thank her. Neglect to mention the fact that I thought they had gone bankrupt/robbed the living daylights out of me and that I had hired hitmen to take out every single one of them.
Don't want to upset the applecart.

Just have to wait for the castle to confirm with us now. But before they can confirm with us, they have to confirm with

Rebekah that the confirmation has been confirmed. Or something like that. All sounds very confusing and I'll try not to worry about it too much. Rebekah should know by next week. I have given them until Thursday to let me know. At least I have in my head. In reality I will just wait.
And sulk.
Probably.
And drink.
Definitely.


## 30 June

No news.
Am not worried.
Maybe a little anxious, but not worried.
Greg AWOL again. Says I've become unbearable.
Have not. Am lovely as always.


## 2 July

Have just realised that I have been trying to book this wedding for almost two months now, and so far all I have done is buy the dress.
Not very good progress.
Begin to panic.


## 3 July

qwertyuioplkjhgfdsazxcvbnm. This is what my life has become. I am a dribbling grey mess that shies away from sunshine and seek solace in a computer. Have become computer nerd. Can you be a computer nerd if you don't know anything about computers? What did people do before the internet came along? How did they organize things? How did they research? How did they shop? How do you book a wedding without using the internet?

Internet good.

Outside world bad.


## 4 July

*17.19*

Oh woe is me! And woe betide anyone who crosses my path! Why does life always throw a spanner in the works? Why do things never run smoothly? Why do I have to organise absolutely bloody everything? It's not fair. I have to arrange the wedding. The reception. The flights. The honeymoon. The internal travel in Italy. The wedding entertainment. The car hire. The guests travel arrangements. The food. The cake (am having Thorntons Celebration cake, can't stand wedding cake and it costs a sodding fortune anyway). And finally the budget.

It's not fair. I didn't ask for any of this.

Will tell Greg that I'm not playing any more. Do not want to do this on my own. He hasn't done a thing to help. Selfish pig.

*18.07*

Greg has just pointed out that I asked for *all* of this. I don't believe I asked for *all* of this. I think I asked for a nice little wedding in Italy with close family and friends. I did *not* ask for stomach ulcer. Have got one anyway. And a headache.

Needless to say there is no sodding news.

I give up, I don't want to get married.

*18.18pm*
Greg has just asked if he can have that last comment in writing. Should I be worried that he said that?

*19.17*
Just finished burying Greg beneath the patio.
Again.
Pesky thing keeps digging himself back up.


## 6 July

DAMMMNNNNN!!!!!
Why?
Why me?
What did I do?
I give money to charity.
I help old ladies across the road.
I'm even polite to Mormons when they come knocking.
Can't even be arsed to write down what's happened. Or *not* happened as the case appears to be. Will find Greg and take it out on him. Need to get shovel so I can dig him up again.


## 7 July

Wasn't in the mood to go over the boring details yesterday. So, here we are, over two months later and no wedding booked. Rebekah has been very helpful, she has explained that it takes time in Italy to get things confirmed, but the people in the castle have *finally* been in touch with her.
We *can* have the castle. Yay!
However, the wedding service will have to be at 3pm which is fine. The reception can be in the grounds, and forecourt

afterwards with candles as requested, which is also fine. The reception must begin at 3.30pm and *must* be over at 4.30pm. YAY! An hour to have my wedding reception! Hurrah!

The reason I have such a paltry amount of time is because a group of wine tasters are visiting to taste some wine (naturally). This is not so fine. Why can't they just go to Threshers to taste wine for God's sake?

Still, not to worry, I have a back-up plan. I tell Rebekah that we like the look of the villa, and she has said that she will contact them and see if it is available. She will be in touch.

Oh God. Here we go again.

## 13 July

*10.33*
Am not stupid pathetic superstitious person so don't give a stuff about the date.

*10.37*
Have just made sign of cross. Am stupid pathetic superstitious person and do give a stuff about the date.

*10.43*
Log onto email. Really don't see the point, but do it anyway.

*11.00*
Hurrah! Have received an email already!! YAY! For the Lord and his sign-making ways. Am convert! Rebekah has said that we can have the villa, and the reception. It comes to slightly less than the castle. She then mentions that the villa will only accept people on a half-board basis, which is over £100.00 per person per night.

Buggery.

Think this is a lot of money to pay, especially for people

who are travelling to Italy for a wedding. Ask Rebekah if she can ask the villa for a discount. Well not the villa but the people that run it. That was really funny in my head, am going mad. She will, and then she will be in touch. Super!

## 19 July

It's my birthday today.
No news.
Other than the fact it's my birthday. Am meeting Catherine for lunch and then Greg is meeting us later.

*02.43*
Hurrah! Have got two bridesmaids. And thumping head. How the freak did I end up with two bridesmaids?

## 20 July

No news yet. However have become alcoholic bore with a penchant for biting young waiters on the arse, and have two bridesmaids. So it's not all bad news.
Must never drink again.
Very bad.
The whole evening started off very sensibly. Met Catherine and we went for lunch – of the food variety and not liquid.
Progressed onto the liquid stuff as soon as dessert was over and ordered a Cosmopolitan. Then a Margarita.
Then a pitcher of sangria – the weather was very hot and we wanted something that tasted like pop but was actually very alcoholic, so it was the natural choice. Then progressed onto plain old wine. Was very sensible and stuck to white wine. Did not mix grapes. Mixing grapes is stupid. Mixing cocktails and sangria and grapes is not stupid. Not when you're

pissed. By the time Greg joined us I was well and truly pissed and proceeded to tell him how much I lurved him but, didn't he think that the handsome young waiter had the cutest arse and didn't he just want to sink his teeth into it.
He didn't.
Got bored with Greg and his sensible ways so I moved on to Catherine. Hurrah for girls! She *did* find the young waiter's arse very attractive and she *did* want to sink her teeth into it, and fully understood why I wanted to. So there. Told Catherine I loved her. Then asked her to be my bridesmaid. Told her no one else could do the job only her, and by the way I loved her. She said yes! Hurrah! Said a big thank you and asked her if she knew that I loved her.
She did. Had mentioned it before apparently.
Then I went to the loo. While sitting on seat contemplating going to sleep I decided to call Jayne and ask her to be a bridesmaid too. Always have fabulous ideas when pissed and sitting on loo.
Jayne asked me if I knew how late it was.
Was not late. Was ten-thirty something. Then remembered that Jayne is very sensible and goes to bed at ten on work nights. Oops. Still, once she realised why I was calling she would be most honoured.
She was and she agreed to be my bridesmaid. So, now I have gone from having no bridesmaids to having two.


## 23 July

Oh hurrah! Yup!
No news. My life is ruled by the internet and the moon.
Or is it water? Don't know what a Cancerian should be ruled by. Do however know that Cancerians and Taureans are supposed to be a 'match made in heaven'. Greg's a Taurean. He can also be a bit of an arse.

## 31 July

Have started to laugh hysterically.
I have no idea what Greg looks like.
When I'm not using the internet Greg is. Though he uses it at night now, generally into the early hours.
Looking at porn.
Probably.
Why did I say probably? I'm not stupid. Of course he's looking at porn. And *Star Trek*. And role-playing games. He's written a role-playing game.
Shame.
I'm marrying that man.
Shame. Am marrying a nerd that would rather look at sci-fi websites than porn.
Am slightly worried.

## 3 August

Getting very angry indeed.
Have had another pointless argument with my husband-to-be. He has once again stomped off after making his point, leaving me feeling frustrated and voiceless. Idiot. Him. Not me.

## 4 August

Pants! The villa will allow the guests to stay on a half-board basis, but only if we can guarantee filling up every room.
Can't do that. In fact won't do it. Will not be dictated to.
I asked Rebekah if she could tell me the name of the villa,

deciding to go direct to them and cut out the crappy middleman/woman/person.

She wouldn't tell me. So I asked her where it was, thinking I could find it online.

She wouldn't tell me.

Pooh!

She is a wise woman.

Don't know what to do. Need to talk it over with Greg, but he isn't home yet. Probably working. He's been working a lot of overtime recently, and when he gets home he's too tired to talk. I used to look forward to seeing him, but sometimes when I hear his key go in the lock, I feel a knot of anxiety tighten in my stomach and avoid talking to him.

We don't seem to be communicating much lately.

There is something not quite right. I can't talk to him any more without feeling afraid. I know he would never physically hurt me, but he gets so angry and he shouts me down. I hate shouting and he knows it.

The argument we had the other day was because I accidentally broke a wine glass. He became very angry, slammed out of the house and didn't come home for several hours. When he did he wouldn't look at me or talk to me, he just went into the study and locked the door. He ignored my knocks and calls and told me go away.

He didn't come to bed until three o'clock in the morning.

All because of a wine glass?

I didn't let him see that I had been crying, not that it would make any difference to him. I'd rather die than let him see me cry.

He'd rather die than see me cry.

The following day I bought another wine glass at the grand price of five pounds and left it on dining table completed with price tag. When he came home he apologised and said he was stressed.

I feel sick, I can't sleep and have lost a lot of weight. I feel trapped, I feel empty, I feel lonely.

I feel afraid.

I'm afraid to act, because I'm afraid of the consequences. How can you discuss something with someone who refuses to talk, and then resorts to shouting in order to get a point across? And who then storms off to God knows where. What do I do?

*01.35*

Greg finished work three and a half hours ago.

He isn't home yet. He is my best friend, but I don't know who he is any more. What are we doing to each other?

*01.42*

What should I do?

How should I handle this?

I don't want to be shouted down, but I know that we need to discuss things.

God I hate that phrase. And 'we need to talk'. Pant girly thing to say.

*01.44*

Where is he? I wish I could stop crying. I hate myself for being so weak. Have I been doing the bucket of sand thing again?

I suspect so.

How long has this been going on? Why have I been ignoring it?

*01.57*

When did the wedding become more important to me than my relationship with Greg? Do I still have a relationship? Do I still want a relationship, let alone a marriage? Not if this is how it's going to be.

*02.06*
Perhaps it's my fault. Perhaps I should spend less time thinking about the wedding. Perhaps I have shut Greg out.
Won't think about the wedding, will concentrate on other things. That's it; I'm not going to think about it.
What wedding?
Hurrah, that was easy.

*02.13*
Still no sign of Greg. No phone call either. He always calls if he's going to be excessively late. I'm beginning to worry now.
Where is he?
I'll try to sleep and tomorrow I won't talk about the wedding, or think about it, I'll concentrate on spending time with Greg.


## 5 August

*12.00*
He came home after four in the morning and stank of beer. I don't know who he is anymore. I pretended to be asleep.

*13.00*
Can't do it. I can't 'not think' about the wedding. Don't think that is grammatically correct, but I know what I mean.
How did I exist before this? Was my life ever simple?
I think it was.
A long time ago.
Have just sent an email to Rebekah telling her that we can't have the villa.
Have told her that we want the date to stay the same, and we still want Tuscany.
Fortunately she is very good and has a very good feel about

what we (I) want and I believe that she will be able to find somewhere.

Everything she has suggested so far has been exactly what we want.

She is going away on holiday for a few weeks, so she won't be around for a few weeks. Perfect timing.

Now all I have to do is wait until she gets back, which is on Sunday 19 August.

*17.00*

Greg and I are doing that very adult thing that people do when neither wants to admit they're in the wrong: the non-talking while actually talking thing. Am very grown up and behaving like an adult about to be married. Perhaps I should apologise for a quiet life. The grown up thing to do would be to ask him if I've done anything wrong, but I'm tired and I don't have the energy to defend myself when he starts shouting. So I'll just ignore it and wait for things to get better, I'm sure they will.

**11 August**

Hurrah!

Have just booked the reception for when we return from the honeymoon.

Am having two receptions!

Hurrah!

Get to wear frock twice!

Have also requested quotes from various marquee companies asking for quotes. Also looking at caterers. And salsa bands. And murder mystery companies. And barn dance companies. And BBQ companies. And outdoor toilet providers. And psychiatrists. And divorce lawyers.

41

Can't do this any more. Need a life of my own. Am going to run away.


## 12 August

Ran away! Ran as far as the off-licence. The man in there keeps giving Greg sympathetic looks. Think he thinks I'm an alcoholic.
I'm not.
Yet.
Am working on it.


## 19 August

*10.03*
Today's the day! She's back! Will assume that she has not had time to send an email to me yet.

*10.15*
Will check anyway. Give her the benefit of the doubt.

*10.25*
Darn! No email. Maybe she isn't working today. Will send her an email and ask her to contact me ASAP.

*10.56*
Greg has told me to 'leave the poor girl alone', she's only just returned from her holiday after all.

## 20 August

I'm sure she's back now. Can't believe that I'm not the number-one priority. Maybe she'll be in touch tomorrow.
Greg has been very quiet.
I've asked him if he's okay, he just told me to leave him alone. When I questioned him further he told me to stop hassling him and then walked out.
He's been doing a lot of that lately. If I follow him he gets quite nasty. He's never been nasty before, but sometimes he looks at me as if he hates me.
I'm sure it's just nerves.

## 21 August

Rushed home. Nothing. No email. Then again I'm sure Rebekah is scouring the whole of Tuscany for the various venues right at this very moment. In fact I'm doubly sure that as I am typing these very words she has secured me a once in a lifetime-fairytale-venue, and is haggling the price on my behalf . . . I'm sure she is.
I hope she is.
Bet she's not.
She probably hates me now because I keep hassling her. Should have listened to Greg. Think I'll go to bed early. Best to sleep rather than fret and make angry phone calls. I won't think about it.

**23 August**

*11.12*
Couldn't sleep because I kept thinking about it. Got up at
6.00am to check my emails. Nothing. I'm in a bit of quan-
dary. Do I call Rebekah again? Shall I email her?
Shall I leave it for a few days . . . hmmm.
**IT'S BEEN NEARLY FOUR MONTHS!!!!**
I'm sure she won't mind if I call her again. In fact I know
she won't, she never does – she is very helpful – and she
does know exactly what I want, and she did say not to worry.
So, maybe I shouldn't worry.

*12.00*
Am worried. Can't help it. Perhaps there will be an email
when I return from work?
Yes. Of course there will . . .

*12.05*
I asked Greg last night what song he would play at my
funeral, if I died before he did. He said, 'Hey-Ho the Witch
is Dead'. Am now worried about that too.

**24 August**

After much soul-searching and guilt-ridden angst, I decided
to bite the bullet and call Rebekah. I planned to tell her
that I had forgotten about her going on holiday and please
forgive, but while she was on the phone could she tell me
whether or not she'd organised my wedding. Or words to
that effect. So, I dialled the number. The Italian version of
the posh BT bird told me something I didn't understand so

I hung up and tried again. This time it rang and on the second ring was answered.

By a man.

Frig.

Still, I had managed to get this far and I was determined to battle on. So I asked to speak to Rebekah. There was a brief pause. Then the phone was put down.

Undeterred I called again.

Posh Italian BT bird again.

I dialled again.

It was answered after the second ring. This time I decided to speak Italian. I can only order wine in Italian, say my name and tell people that I'm on my honeymoon, all of which I believe will come in handy – eventually. So I ordered a small red wine, told him my name was Chloe and that I was on my honeymoon. It did the trick. After a brief pause he spoke in English, and his English was far, far superior to my Italian, but still not hot.

'Ah Chloe, you are Chloe!'

I took it as a great sign.

Rebekah had obviously told him about me! YAY!

I told him that yes I was Chloe. And I was calling because I was concerned about my marriage. Or lack of it.

He told me not to worry, that things have a way of 'playing with themselves'.

I asked him if he knew anything about my marriage, had he heard anything, could he tell me anything, was Rebekah there?

No. No Rebekah. No he hadn't heard anything, no he didn't know anything, but why was I concerned?

I found him very understanding and very easy to talk to, plus he had a very sexy voice and he had the whole Italian thang going for him, so I decided to have a chat. I told him I was concerned because my marriage wasn't going any-where, I had been waiting months, and I was stuck in limbo with no action. He told me that marriages take time, that you have to be patient, and if I couldn't be patient, he had a great libido and was willing to show me some action.

Hmm. Not what I was after but at least he wasn't shouting at me. As shocking as that was, I had a brief stirring and I believe my nipples may have gone hard. He did have a wonderful voice.

But it was wrong.

He may sound very sexy, and he may be Italian and as such I was certain he could do a thing or two with hard nipples, but he was a thousand miles away and was married.

And I told him as much.

He then told me that he had been married for almost 35 years and that his sister-in-law was called Rebekah. I asked him if his Rebekah arranged marriages. He said the only one she had arranged was between himself and his wife years ago and that he still hadn't forgiven her, but did I still need help with my libido.

I put the phone down.

I still have no idea what Rebekah's telephone number is. I dialled correctly. She must have given me the wrong number.

Phones can be so deceiving. Amazingly I now have the most pleasurable sensation when wearing T-shirts without my bra. And *that* hasn't happened in a *long* time.


## 5 September

*10.00*

Still no news about the wedding.

Greg and I on the other hand haven't been out for weeks, we hardly eat together, we can barely say two words without arguing and he uses any excuse to leave the house.

He hasn't spoken to me for that past three days and I have no idea why.

Probably because I went out with Catherine the other night and didn't get back until late. I wanted him to know how it felt to worry.

Ha!

Silly me.

The git was asleep when I got home, oblivious to everything.

*11.15*

Wonder if it's because I forgot to tape *Buffy* the other night. Actually didn't forget to tape it at all, I recorded over it the following night with *Eastenders*, but I told him I'd forgotten to tape it.

I'm not too hot on taping things. Something always goes wrong. I once taped over his collection of *Red Dwarf*. Wasn't my fault, how was I supposed to know that it was a British sci-fi masterpiece? Thought *Space 1999* was the British sci-fi masterpiece.

Eek.

How do I know that? Oh God. Have become geek. Shit. Bet I look like one.

No wonder Greg doesn't want to spend any time with me, I probably look like Olive from *On the Buses* – think all female sci-fi fans look like Olive from on the buses.

He was actually rather sweet when that happened and laughed at me and told me not to worry, he could always buy the official tapes.

Ahh. Greg used to be lovely. He's a total arse now though. This wedding has really changed him. I don't know what's come over him. It's as though he only speaks to me when necessary, and he has taken to locking himself away in the study, looking at his little sci-fi sites probably.

I need to look on the internet though, and check my email, but I don't want to disturb him. Oh, who the hell am I kidding? It's about time I admitted to myself the reason I won't confront Greg.

I'm scared.

Too scared to talk to him.

I'm too scared to ask him if I can use the internet, because I know he'll just sigh and go out and I won't know what time he'll come home. Or where he goes. God I sound pathetic!

I used to be so strong. I used to stand up for myself, but how can I defend myself when there's no official battle? There's just a stony silence where there used to be love.

I've lost all interest in the wedding. I've lost interest in everything. I don't have the energy to care anymore.

*12.15*
Wonder if I've had an email yet?

## 13 September

*13.00*
The man I fell in love with is slowly disappearing and I don't know what to do.

I have no idea who he is, I have no idea where he is, and I have absolutely no idea who I am. I'm a crazy hell bride with no time for anyone or anything.

*14.07*
Bugger it. Am crying. Big fat 'it's a shame for me' tears. Have no idea why. Am silly, that's why. I'm a silly stupid cow who feels sorry for herself.

*14.33*
I feel so alone. And I am never lonelier than when Greg is lying next to me, we are together and yet oceans apart.

## 14.46

I know this situation can't continue. I have to tackle Greg, but part of me doesn't want to. Part of me would rather run away. Yup, that's it, I'll run off to a paradise island and fall in love with a priest who'll leave the clergy for me – even though there is very little point in the clergy leaving the clergy just for sex these days – they're all at it. But anyway that's what I'd prefer to do. The arse-aching truth of the matter though, is that I *have* to confront him.

And I'm shit scared.

## 14.17

Then again, perhaps running away and having an affair is the better option.

That or the ostrich impression. I'm very good at doing the 'ostrich'. Some of my worst situations have been avoided while being pink and one-legged. Or is that a flamingo? Flamingos are pretty. Much rather be a flamingo than an ostrich.

Am not very good at confrontations. I either make a hash of the situation and forget my point, or just agree for a quiet life. But usually after making someone cry. Or making myself cry.

## 14.47

Could be my fault I suppose. I can be difficult, and I always challenge people, even if I agree with them, I just can't stand complacency, so every now and then I'll make some-one defend their point of view, just to be awkward.

Greg hates it when I do that.

## 15.00

Apparently I'm impossible to live with.

My mum says so, and Greg says so – though he's managed to live with me relatively stress-free for this long.

*15.07*

Then again he does always try to sell me back to my parents every time we visit them.

Have always assumed it was a joke. Hope it's a joke. Not very nice hearing your husband-to-be negotiating a sell-back deal with your parents. Also not very nice when said parents look terrified at the thought of getting prodigal daughter back and utter words akin to 'we remember what she's like'.

Am nice girl.

Am a good girl.

Have opinions that's all. And I'll be shagged if I'm going to keep them to myself just so other people can have a quiet life. Greg says that life with me is far from boring. Have always taken it as a compliment. Maybe it isn't. Oh what the hell do I know?

Yup. Quiet lives are boring.

*16.58*

Wish I had a quiet life. Maybe I am impossible. I knew this would be my fault. Should have known really. It's usually my fault. I don't mean to do it, it's just my way. Whatever 'it' is. I never do get to find out – I'm just aware that something is wrong. And I've usually done 'it'. Pants.

*18.00*

No!

No. No. No. No!!

This time it *isn't* my fault.

Hah!

This time I want to know what's wrong with *him*. I have to speak to him when he gets home, and I'm terrified. I'm a big fat coward.

No I'm not. I'm a good girl I am.

*20.30*

Greg finished work at three o'clock and he's not home yet.
Again. This is becoming a habit.

*21.57*

I am between anger, concern and despair. I have no idea
what to do.
There are track marks in the floorboards where I have
paced up and down wondering what I should do. Why would
he do this to me? Would he do this? I can't believe that he
would, not Greg, not the man I know and love.
Is he still the man I know and love?

*22.06*

What could I have done that is so bad he can't talk to me,
and would rather avoid me?
Maybe he doesn't want to get married. It was his sodding
idea! I was leaving! Okay I was leaving because I couldn't be
in a relationship that had no definite future, but it wasn't an
underhand nasty little plot just to get my own way. I was
really truly going to leave. I had my bags packed and
everything.
Wish I'd gone now – I can't stand this any more. Why do we
have to play mind games all the time? When did crying
become a part of my daily routine?

*22.13*

Maybe I should have the conversation in my head.
Yes that's what I'm going to do.
Here goes:
'We need to talk.'
'Piss off.'
'Righty-ho then.'
There I go! That wasn't too difficult, now all I need to do is
not talk to me for two days and I'm done.

*23.33*

I can't sleep but at least the weight loss will still be on course.

Yay!

I have rehearsed a thousand times what I will say to Greg, but I know that when I see him my emotions will get the better of me and I'll have an attack of verbal diarrhoea, as per usual. I can't help but wonder if this is intentional. Maybe he *wants* me to confront him, perhaps this is his way of handling whatever problem he has.

*23.47*

Have done the unforgivable. I called his work to see if he was still there.

He wasn't, he left at three. His colleagues told me to try the pub facing work, so I did.

He *was* in there but left at about seven. I asked who with, but the landlord said he couldn't say. He sounded cagey, almost as though he'd been put in an awkward situation. Feel nausea welling up inside.

*01.25*

He has just come home. I can hear him downstairs opening cupboards and making food as though nothing is wrong.

Where is the man I agreed to marry? Where am I? When did I become so afraid?

I know what I need to do but I am paralysed with fear, but my fear is not of the consequences. It's of his reaction. I really am afraid of him. Shit that's a scary thing to admit to. I feel as though I've been slapped across the face with an iron bar. How long have I been afraid? What exactly am I afraid of?

I don't think for one minute that he would physically harm me, but the emotional control he has over me is sometimes stupefying. I find myself backing down just to avoid another spiteful slanging match. I gauge his mood when he comes home and feel myself relax when he's the old Greg, and I feel myself die a little each time he ignores me and locks himself away. I know I have to talk to him, but the thought makes me sick with fear.

Where does he go?

If I follow him in a desperate attempt to get my point across, he will shout, he will push me, and his face will contort and he will look at me with pure hatred and tell me that I have *made him* the way he is.

*01.49*

Is it really all my fault? Is it? Perhaps it is.

Sod it.

*02.07*

Wish we lived in France – killing him would be so much easier. Must hide diary, can't have him reading that! I am going to tackle the situation head on. I will not be bullied.

## 15 September

*05.47*

My life is turning into a soap opera. And not a very good one. I wouldn't bloody watch it.

Well I might, but only to see the Evil Tossing Bastard (Greg) get his comeuppance from the Sweet and Beautiful heroine (that would be me – I am sweet). In my soap opera the heroine would confront Evil Tossing Bastard, and he would twirl his thin black moustache and squint evilly into the camera, before attempting to silence her forever, at which point Mr Handsome Dashing Totally In Control I'll Save You My Dear (position to be filled) dashes onto screen and saves the day, and more importantly, the Sweet and Beautiful heroine.

Real life, however, doesn't go quite as well.

So the Not Quite Beautiful heroine decided to speak to Evil Tossing Bastard or at least she tried to. She asked him what time he came home. He said, 'Late.' She asked him where he had been. He said, 'Out.' She asked him with whom. He said, 'With friends.' She asked him if they could talk – he said, 'What about?'

So far so bad!

Handling the situation like real adults.

As per usual I was getting nowhere so I changed tactics, and told him that we *needed* to talk. He said, 'Go on then. Talk.' And he looked me directly in the eyes and defied me to question him.

It was a warning sign. Don't do warning signs. Never ever see warning signs.

I certainly didn't see any in this situation, so I ploughed on and questioned him, and questioned him, and then questioned him some more. I ignored the throbbing thick vein that was pulsing at the side of his head. I was aware of it, but I ignored it. Am good at that. Ignoring things is my forte.

I also ignored the bile that began to rise in my stomach. I went on and on and I played right into his hands. He said he felt trapped, he said I was unreasonable.

Was I?

Wasn't he?

Aren't we all at times?

He shouted and screamed, and told me I was destroying his life. He said he was sick of hearing all about the wedding, that he had no interest in the wedding, that I had become boring, and that he was sick to death of being ignored. I pointed out that I have on several occasions tried to include him in the wedding arrangements but he has never shown any interest.

He didn't like that. 'Cause I was right.

Ha!

So, like the evil tosser he is, he pushed me away, walked off and refused to listen to me.

So far so predictable.

Except this time I refused to be bullied, and I didn't cower away from him. I followed him and questioned him more and more. I pushed him and pushed him and somewhere deep inside a perverse pleasure was satisfied in seeing his rage rise, so I pushed on, and on and on. Until he grabbed me around the throat pushed me into the wall and lifted his balled fist to me.

He didn't hit me.

He didn't have to.

This was the man I loved.

The man I had shared my dreams with. He was my future and yet as he stood in front of me with his fist raised, I felt that future slip away, there was a shift of emotion and a part of me closed down. Perhaps it will never be rebuilt.

## 07.10

When do dreams end and reality bite? How do we get to that point in life where choices are taken from us and existence is imposed?

Yesterday I had a wedding to plan, a future, I had hope, and yet it all vanished when I looked into the eyes of the man I loved, the man who had been my soulmate, my companion and my best friend, and I saw nothing reflected but hatred and rage, and I realised that I no longer had any choices.

The world I had planned has vanished and reality has taken the place of dreams. The fairytale ending, and the happy ever after, they belong to another life. The sunset has faded and real life has begun. And I have to start living in the real world and stop being so bloody optimistic.

The man I love has disappeared, I don't know how to get

him back, and I don't sodding care. How's that for reality?
It's pants, that's what. I will stop thinking about it. I'll push
it to the back of my mind and think about it another day,
when I can cope.
Wonder if it's too early for alcohol?

*11.23*
I can't tell my mum what has happened, she'll bloody kill
him. Shit. So will my brother. Shit. And my dad. I'll probably
just dance on his corpse.

*11.57*
I've spent the past few minutes staring out of the window,
trapped between the now and the yesterday. I can't stop
thinking about what happened and how I handled the
situation. Perhaps I pushed him. I *know* I pushed him. The
question is, would he have gone any further, would he have
actually hit me? What would I have done if he had?
Would I have reacted in the same way?
I just stood looking up at him and watched as his anger and
rage gave way to shock and disgust, and I walked away. I
ignored his pleas for forgiveness; I froze when he touched
me and asked me to stay. I laughed when he asked if we
could talk.
Within minutes I had packed a small bag and I walked away.
I have left my home, my security, my identity and the man I
love behind me, I have an uncertain future before me, and
nothing but a gaping hole where my heart used to be.
What the fuck have I done?!!
I am back at my parents, in my old bedroom, and I feel like
a twelve-year-old again. Though I admit it is rather nice
being waited on hand and foot. Mum even knocked on my
door earlier and came in with a lollipop.
Am twelve.
Shit I hope not. I had no breasts when I was twelve, I wore a

trainer bra thinking it taught breasts how to grow. Took two years before it worked. Still, I've made up for lost time, have rather ample bosom now. Show a man a pair of breasts and he's anyone's – at least for the night.

*17.30*
Hurrah! Is time for alcohol and chocolate. Will comfort eat until I'm sick and drink until I sing.

*17.55*
Went for a snoop in my brother's old bedroom. He's a bit of a boffin. Found a book on theology. Have decided I will become intellectual expert on God.

*18.40*
How did I get here? Where will I go? What will happen to me? Why?
Book is good. A bit confusing but still it makes one think. In the grand scheme of things, I am no more than an ant. A teeny-weeny ant, scurrying around the earth getting on with its business. Ahhh. Would have been an ant in a wedding dress with a sparkly tiara.
Bless.
Would have had a little ant party as well, and invited lots of other teeny ants. Would have got drunk on ant beer and done a little ant congo.

*19.20*
Maybe that's what ants are doing when they scurry back and forth to their nests. Bet they're not working at all. Bet they've all gone to an ant wedding, got pissed on ant beer and are doing the congo. Must never pour boiling water and bleach on ants ever again. Bummer of a way to end a wedding.

*01.45*
Greg has called three times, I have told my mum to tell him I'm not here. I don't want to speak to him, I don't want to hear his voice. I don't want to think about him. I am trying to get by, hour by hour. I will not cry, and if I do I will never let anyone see me cry. I don't think I have any tears left inside me. Have oodles of wine though, and a bit of blue stuff I found in the back of the cupboard that tasted like mints.

*02.00*
I will never again show any weakness.
I will never again be vulnerable.
I will never again trust in 'happiness'.
I will never again be sober.

*02.30*
I can feel a change inside that I feel is irreversible. A part of me has died. Or perhaps evolved.
Or sobered up a bit.

*03.15*
I fell asleep, dreamt of Greg, I woke up crying.
How do I stop loving him?
Why has this happened?
What did I do?
I screamed a combination of swear words into my pillow and invented several more.
It didn't help.
My life is crap and I'll never be loved.
Except by my parents, and they don't count.
I don't mean that in a nasty way.
It is now 03.27 and I have opened a bottle of imported vodka that is 100 per cent proof, and I don't give a shit. Why

58

should I? WHY IS THIS HAPPENING TO ME??? What did I do that was so *bad*?

I don't even eat red meat for God's sake. And I love *all* animals, and small children.

Not over keen on babies though. They don't do anything except poo and scream. And stare at you as though you're a piece of shit.

God, even babies hate me.

*03.43*

I will not, ever, ever, ever, listen to or sing:
   a)  All By Myself
   b)  I Will Survive

If I do I'm going to shoot myself. Or Greg. That's it. I'll shoot Greg.

*03.56*

Need a gun.

And a life.

And Greg.

No I don't!!!!

Am a bit pissed. Maybe I should call Greg. Stuff him. Into a six-foot casket preferably. WHY HAS THIS HAPPENED???

Maybe because there is someone totally and utterly perfect for me who isn't a tit, arse or any other part of the human anatomy that sounds rude and funny.

Like penis.

Greg is a penis.

And not a big one either.

Am really rather drunk.

I'm sure there is someone out there who will like me for just being me, who won't *want* me to change.

*04.07*

Well, perhaps they'll want me to change a teeny bit but

not forever, just for a social occasion or something that only lasts for a few hours. I don't really do 'social'. Actually I do. But I usually end up a bit squiffy and tell appalling jokes, and disclose rather too much information about myself.

Such as the fact that Roy Wood sat on my face when I was a child. I was at a house party and he was there. Think I should add that I was asleep on the sofa at the time and he didn't see me. Titbits like that don't always go down well. Especially if I'm at works 'do' and having to look after a children's author. They're rather sensitive types. Actually I also 'do' social if it's a rather swanky affair with big frocks, champagne and canapés.

I rather do social then.

*04.87*
Can't see to tell the time properly. Have topped the vodka back up with water and tried to reseal the cap. I'm sure they won't notice.

*04.93*
Hrrah! have invented new time system. I shall call it Chloe-ien Time. Have reopened vodka. Tastes like boiled pants.

*05.95*
GO ON NOW GO! WALK OUT THE DOOR! JUST TURN AROUND NOW . . .


**16 September**

Had about three hours sleep.
Woke up with eyes that looked and felt as though they had been rubbed in salt and hair that Anita Dobson would be proud of. I suspected that my breath had the scent of an

arse-licking kitten and while in my vodka-induced sleep I had dribbled onto my pyjamas.

And I didn't care.

I was back at home and home is where the pampering is. I went downstairs without bothering to remove the crusty yellow stuff from my eyes and walked straight into Greg.

Shit.

Ran back upstairs on the pretext of not wanting to talk to him, while secretly cursing the fact that I looked like an extra from *Thriller*. I had no make up, no brush and no deodorant. Didn't pack very well. So I did the only thing I could – I had a shower. When I finished, I dragged a comb through my hair and left most of it trapped between the teeth. Hurrah! Now I was smelly *and* bald.

I rubbed toothpaste on my teeth, and didn't notice that a large quantity of it gathered at the crease of my mouth.

But at least I wasn't bald and smelly. I was bald and looked as though I had rabies. Which I only realised when I looked in mirror later.

When I walked into the bedroom Greg was sitting on the edge of the bed.

He looked like shit.

He had huge grey bags beneath his eyes and his sockets were red raw. I just stood staring at him, and felt a wealth of emotions. I'm sure that somewhere among them was love, but it was vying for its position among revulsion, concern and a deep longing to be held.

I walked away without saying anything and went into my parents' room before the first tear fell. He didn't follow me and he didn't see me cry.

He left.

When I returned to my room with its memories and child-hood hopes, there was a letter on the bed. I broke down before I even opened it. There would be no going back, no matter what happened. I would always remember and I would always be afraid, and the decision I made now would seal my future.

I opened the letter and read it slowly through my tears.

He was sorry.

He was confused.

He was scared.

His emotions were overpowering and beyond his control and he was afraid. I could be overwhelming, I could be stubborn, I could be infuriating, but he knew it was no excuse. There could be no excuse for his actions.

He had spent the whole night going over the situation in his head, and he was ashamed of himself, he was shocked and afraid and he had absolutely no idea that he could react like that.

Could I forgive him?

He loved me, I was his support, his 'rock', and only I could help him get through this, he couldn't imagine life without me. Could we talk and discuss things? Would I go home?

I put the letter away and went to sleep. Sleep always helps, it obliterates everything.

Sleep and alcohol.

## 18 September

Sleeping fitfully.

I keep dreaming of Greg.

Good dreams of how life used to be.

I still haven't spoken to him.

What would I say? That I forgive him? Forgive him for what? For being pushed to the very edge? Hadn't I done the pushing? Wasn't I also to blame? Doesn't it take two people to cause an argument as explosive as ours? Wasn't I always the one that carried things too far, that went on and on until I was finally satisfied that I had been heard? How would

I react if the situation had been reversed? There are far too many questions that I can't answer myself, and if I don't know the answers how can Greg?

When a relationship is on the brink of destruction surely one of the parties involved should have the answers that could rescue it. That someone is generally me, and the only answer I have at them moment is 'yes mother I am freakin' cold thank you very much.' Why can't old people use central heating properly? It's either too hot or too damn cold. Have icicles hanging from my nose. Too cold to write, several fingers have already snapped off.

My mother is Ebenezer Scrooge.

### 15.00

Am now nice and toasty, fingers in full working order and I'm having one of the high moments in life when you believe that everything will work out. We will get through this, we will be married, we will be happy. Sometimes a relationship has to face near destruction before it can continue, and when it does, it is stronger, happier, and more open. That's what's happening.

I know that a lot of our problems stem from my stubborn inability to let arguments drop. I won't give in until we have both had an equal say. I should learn to let things be, and recognise the fact that not everyone likes to talk things through.

Some things need to be left alone. Some things need to be forgotten.

### 15.45

Does that excuse his actions though? Shit. Nice optimistic feeling is being replaced with a life is wank feeling. Must cling desperately to the hope that things will be okay.

*15.56*
Pants. Hope gone. The future looks a bit grey. A pair of grey pants is what my future holds. Will be a spinster with hundreds of cats and smell of cat food.
Shit. Perhaps I already do.

*16.10*
I am writing utter drivel and trash in this diary. I think I'm writing just for the sake of it. It fills a gap.
No I'm not. I'm using as a sounding board, a way of working through my emotions in the hope of reaching a decision. Hurrah! I rock! Oprah has nothing on me. Perhaps I could be a chat-show host, think I would be very good at that, very sympathetic with all the guests, I can 'uh-uh' and 'hmm' along with the best of them and then come out with utter drivel. For utter drivel, please see above.
Chloe what are you doing?
Going mad that's what.
Terribly mad.
GET A GRIP!!

*16.45*
Uh-oh! Grip lost on life. Grip now round neck of wine bottle.

*18.00*
Have not had any wine. I opened it, but then stuffed the cork back in. I must be very sensible, I have to make a decision, and I must have a clear head. People have been very supportive, and they have all in their own way tried to help and offer me support, but I know that it doesn't matter what anyone else thinks or says, I have to follow my heart.
Of course my heart has to be taped back together before I can follow it, but once it's back in shape, I *will* follow it. No matter where it leads.

## 28 September

I met Greg yesterday, and I have to say I looked fabulous. Or if not fabulous it was at least a vast improvement on the crazed rabid dog with bed hair that he saw last. I went shopping for clothes beforehand and bought a little red number and that boosted not only my confidence but also my breasts.

Boys are suckers for breasts. Don't get it. They're just wobbly bits of flesh with pointy things. Ah well, at least I know my audience.

We met at a little riverside bar and I made sure I was the first to arrive. For some reason I didn't want him to buy me a drink, I didn't want to feel ingratiated, but I figured that a refusal would set the whole evening off on the wrong footing, so arrived early and bought a huge glass of wine.

True to form he was ten minutes late. He rushed in full of apologies and looking sheepish. He looked like the old Greg, and I felt a lurch of familiarity and love. He was open and unsure of himself and a little awkward, but most of all he had the old look in his eyes. The look that told me he was pleased not only to see me, but of what he saw. I was wanted once again, I was needed and a part of the iceberg that surrounded my heart melted.

When he hugged me I tried to hug him back, but it was awkward, almost incestuous, and I found that I couldn't, not at first. But then I felt his arms around me and the closeness of his body and I breathed in the familiar scent of him and felt the warmth radiating from his open jacket and for the briefest of moments the past was eradicated and we were together again. The rest of the world was simply a place we had to inhabit in order to exist.

I have no idea how long we stood there holding each other – clinging to each other – lost in nostalgia, remembering how things used to be, how we used to love, how we used to play, how we used to *go* together, and how we used to dream the same dreams, but somewhere, lost within that desperate moment, a decision was made, and I have no idea where that decision will lead. I am afraid of my choice, but then I would have been afraid of any choice. And I would rather risk the unknown than spend a lifetime of 'what ifs'. So after an evening of tears and talk, the wedding is back on.

I am back home, in my own house, with its comforting fires and its half finished kitchen. Except it feels a little less homely than it used to. Somehow the fire is not quiet as welcoming. Somehow Greg and I are not quite as relaxed with each other.

I'm sure it will pass.

## 3 October

The oomph has left me. The oomph has oomph-ed and off-ed. What's the point anyway? Surely the marriage is more important than the wedding?

Yes. It is. Of course it is.

Have not heard a thing from Rebekah, and I don't really care. Still, it doesn't stop me from having the occasional 'arse-in-hand' moment, but they are few and far between and Greg doesn't notice anyway, so 'hurrahs' all round.

He still has no interest in the wedding and whenever I waft something beneath his nose he grunts and says that's nice. Wafted a picture of me shagging a donkey under his nose once, just to gauge his reaction. 'Hhhm that's nice. Make a lovely centre piece.' That bit's made up, but it could be true. Except I've never had sex with a donkey. Or any other animal. Well actually several animals, but they've all been of the human, male variety.

Should have shagged a donkey instead.

Anyway, was at work, and on the internet allegedly looking for author venues but in reality I was having another 'woe is me' moment, so I typed, 'wedding' + 'cheap' + 'UK' into the search engine.

It bought back a rather grand looking manor house in Scotland. Daddy comes from Scotland so it's allowed. Granddaddy came from Italy so that was allowed too. I have granddaddy to thank for the smattering of freckles across my nose, which Greg says look like pooh smatterings. Greg's an arse.

I tell myself that they are very cute, in fact when I was little people used to give me ten pence for each freckle. So they're actually quite lucrative. Yay! for Granddaddy!

Anyhow, I called the people at the manor and asked if they could quote me some prices.

I don't do Scottish accents. My Auntie Anne has a very thick Scottish accent and I find myself agreeing with everything she says and smiling at her. She thinks I'm a nutter. So when my call was answered by a woman with a very sweet but very thick Scottish accent it didn't bode well. I asked her how much the hire of the manor was. She said two hundred pounds. Hmm, very cheap, but how many hours did two hundred pounds buy? Would we have to be out after three hours?

Nope.

Two hundred pounds bought us all day. Hurrah! But what's the catch I thought, and then realised that of course they would charge an extortionate fee for food, so I asked her how much the food was.

Whatever she said next I couldn't understand. So I asked her to repeat it. She did. I still couldn't understand. So I asked her to repeat it. She did. What the freak was the woman saying?? She sighed and repeated it again. It sounded very much like 'fifty pounds per head not including wine.' So I said thank you and goodbye. Then spent the next thirty minutes going over the conversation in my head. I then called Auntie Anne in Scotland – have *never* called Auntie Anne – ever, ever, ever, and I doubt she would remember who I was anyway, but I decided it was time to say 'hi' and while I was on the phone I asked her to say 'fifty' and 'fifteen' to me.

She did.

And then she asked who I was.

She'd never heard of me.

Bless her. That story will buzz round the dinner tables of Dundee for a while.

But at least now I knew that there was the strongest possibility that I had mis-heard the lady at the manor house. So I had to call back.

I didn't want to call back and look like a fool so I came up with a plan. I didn't want the woman at the manor to know that it was me so I decided to put on a bit of an accent and pretend to be someone else asking about a wedding. A wedding on the same day as mine. With the same amount of guests. And exactly the same requirements.

Didn't think my plan through very well. That and the fact that I don't really do accents meant that the woman knew it was me. I then pretended that I thought I'd called another manor house in the area, to which she said that there were no other manor houses in the area.

Crap.

I could have either put the phone down or just plodded on. So I plodded on and said I was sorry I didn't know my arse from my elbow and was very confused but while she was on the phone could she please tell me if the cost of food per head was 'fif*teen* or fif*ty*'. Her response could have been either. So I asked her to repeat it.

And then asked her to repeat it again. And every time I asked she repeated herself. She was very calm and very polite, but I still had no idea what she was saying, and I felt a bubble of uncontrollable laughter rise when I asked again if she could please repeat herself. I didn't actually listen to her response because I was too busy laughing, and once I'd started I couldn't stop. Meanwhile, a very patient Scottish woman was shouting her response and breaking down the syllables for me, and emphasising each one.

It really didn't help.

It sounded like Klingon.

I couldn't control my laughter and had tears rolling down my face while she plodded on and tried very hard to shout over me and make me understand her, but I couldn't and this just made me laugh even more. By this time my pretend lunch hour was well and truly over and I really shouldn't have been on the phone or using the internet, at least not for personal use, and my laughing had caught the attention of several people, one of them my boss, who all gathered round my desk to see what was so amusing. I quickly clicked away the image of the manor house, only to reveal a picture of my wedding dress. I was panicking by this time. And sweating.

I shooed everyone away, including my boss, and continued the conversation with my Klingon friend.

Except she was laughing now and we couldn't understand one another and that made us laugh even more. So I said I'd send her an email.

From work of course.

Got home, checked email and she had sent me a response!! Bless the people of the UK and their quick responses!! The cost per head is fifteen pounds.

Hurrah!

Have booked a weekend there to take a look and see what the catch is.

## 30 October

Have been to the manor house. It's fab. Love it. It's a family-run hotel, and they're very friendly, and very helpful and will organise *everything* and only charge for the phone calls.

So I'm having a piper – YAY! And a Scottish dance-type thing – can't remember what they're called.

And a children's puppeteer – don't have anything to say about that other than at least the little people will be quiet for a while.

Also met the minister. He's as mad as a fish.

My wedding day has been set for 6 July 2003.

Am almost happy. Shouldn't I be ecstatic? Push horrible thoughts away – just nerves – that's what people tell me.

So, it's all done and dusted. Nothing left to arrange. No point in keeping a diary any more. At least not for trivial stuff. I'll keep it for the big things, for the exciting events that take place in a marriage.

The future beckons and it's a bright and hazy sunrise that is about to bask the world in its life-giving radiance.

There were no more entries regarding the engagement; there was nothing more to write. Life continued and Greg and I grew more and more distant, and yet neither of us would admit it to the other – we both did the ostrich thing.

And finally, the day itself arrived, and there wasn't a fanfare to be heard. Since the marriage break-up Greg has told me that when he turned to watch me walk down the aisle he felt nothing. Not a thing. He was about to marry his best friend, his sister, but not the woman he loved with a passion.

And I knew . . .

## 6 July

*13.30*
My dress is beautiful. My make-up is perfect. The sun has turned my pale skin light olive. My tiara sparkles against my long dark hair. Chloe looks like a princess.
Yet when I look in the mirror I don't see her. I don't *feel* her.
I feel nothing.
One and a half hours ago I married my best friend. The man I have been with for eight years. The man I have grown with. The man that walks away from me whenever I stand next to him. The man whose smile no longer reaches his eyes. That man said 'I do.'
I suspect he doesn't.


## 29 July

The honeymoon is over.
In truth, the honeymoon didn't begin; it was more like a holiday with a best friend. Someone you go away with but can't wait to get away from, my husband was irritated by me, he was silent and non-responsive, and would often sigh for no reason. I didn't question him; I have learnt not to probe, I know when to question and when to leave things alone.

And I leave things alone in the vain hope that things will get better.

But questions still need to be answered so I simply examine myself and my own actions and I replay events in my mind to try to pinpoint the exact moment he changed, and how I had effected that change, and I withdraw into myself, afraid of upsetting him further.

I cry almost every day. I have never felt so lonely or so desperate.

Who can I talk to, where can I turn?

On the surface we have a perfect marriage, his displays of affection are grand and loving, yet behind closed doors he can be moody and silent, and his anger will flare over the simplest of things and the shouting begins again, and I am reduced to tears, and they only feed his anger.

He hasn't once lifted his hand to me. Not since the last incident, but sometimes I wish he would. Sometimes I wish I had something tangible that I could act upon.

Who has ever left a loving husband simply because he shouts? Who understands a woman that says she can't cope with emotional distress any longer? What is emotional distress anyway? Surely it's a sign of weakness, of failure? Who ever sees beyond what is on the surface? Who has the time to listen to what is being said?

I have tried so many times in so many ways to tell people how I feel. I have joked about my unhappiness in the same way Greg jokes about my looks, or my hair or my conversational skills. I try to tell people that he is just as difficult to live with, only to be reminded of how impossible I am, and Greg will then hold court and entertain people with stories of my actions and my unreasonable behaviour, and I will look at his adoring audience and hope that they see my despair. I will give someone a look and hope desperately that they see me. But they never do. Greg is Greg, he is the joker, he is the man that entertains, the man that brings a group alive, and lately it has been at my expense. He will entertain them with in-depth personal stories, but they are just jokes, amusing anecdotes, he doesn't *mean* anything by them.

My life is a farce, but I am not laughing. Not any more.

And then there are the good times when things are going well. When he is Greg again, and we can laugh and love and enjoy each other's company. Those are the good times and they eradicate the bad and I feel valued and wanted again, I am on a high.

But the high never lasts.

My marriage has not been consummated.

I don't know who I am, or who I used to be; I feel unwanted and unattractive, and I am losing control of my life.


## September

I haven't written in here for such a long time. I remember when I had so much to say, when I was full of so much energy and excitement, but there doesn't seem to be much to say any more.

Life goes on.

Greg is hardly ever home. When he's not working he's out drinking. I hardly ever see him. We don't really go out together any more, which is fine, because I no longer have any desire to go out.

The last time we went out I bored people. Apparently. Greg has told me that I can sometimes 'go on a bit'. He says that I continue talking when in reality I should just shut up because people aren't interested in what I have to say. He put his arms around me and told me that it wasn't my fault, it's just that I need to read the signs; I must realise when people have lost interest in my conversation.

Have always been a bit of a gabbler, but I didn't really think it was that much of a problem.

Apparently it is.

I think that Greg is right though – the last time we went out I hardly spoke and no one seemed to notice. Think I read those signs well enough: am a boring fart.

Thank God Greg still finds me interesting.

Feel like a bit of an idiot now. I wonder how many people I've bored in the past? Ah well, at least I don't bore Greg, not yet anyway.


## October

How very different things look one year on.

This time last year I had booked the venue for my wedding and was so excited, looking forward not only to my marriage but to married life. I can still feel the bubble of excitement and happiness that I felt all those months ago.

And now I am a newly-married woman in a marriage that has no life and no passion. Things are no different.

On the surface, Greg and I are happy. When we do go out we are the perfect example of togetherness. When we are surrounded by our friends and he puts his arm around me and kisses me and tells me that he loves me, I feel myself relax and warm to his words and believe in what he's saying. But then the evening ends and we go home, and he kisses me on the forehead and disappears into the study where he will sit until the early hours of the morning, browsing the internet.

We have still not consummated our marriage.

I have no confidence. Greg says that he cannot look at me in 'that way'. He will not elaborate on what he means, he simply says that I must give him time, I must not push the issue because that just makes it worse for him.

So I live in silence. I withdraw more and more into myself as each day passes. When did I become so repulsive?

I have tried to become more passive and less opinionated, in an attempt to help matters: perhaps that's the problem, maybe it's because I'm too strong-willed.

Perhaps he's right, perhaps I am too forthright.

People often tell me I'm too confident or outspoken, it's never struck me as a bad thing, until now.

Have lost weight and gained a stomach ulcer.

Big YAY for marriage.

Stupid, stupid girl.


## 14 November

Greg is never home.

He no longer calls to say he's working late, he just doesn't come home. We occupy the same house, but different worlds. We have lost touch with one another.

Each week he seems to work more and more overtime, followed by more and more visits to the pub with his shift.

And I experience more and more loneliness.

I am trying harder and harder to make him happy, and the more I try, the more of myself I lose. I hang onto his every word, his expressions, his tone of voice, his demeanour: when I hear his key in the lock I try to pre-guess his mood and am ready with my counter-attack.

My confidence is non-existent. On the surface I haven't changed. People looking at me still think that I am the same Chloe, they think I am happily married, they think I am lucky.

Chloe isn't here any more. I didn't like her. And if I didn't like her, who else would? Who would ever find her interesting? Who could ever cope with her? Who will ever find her attractive?

Who cares?
Shit.
Have started to talk in the third person.
Am mad.


## 15 November

Hurrah!
Pants to what I said yesterday! Have date with my husband!
A real live date! He said that he realises he's been doing a
lot of overtime and thinks we should go out to catch up with
one another. Hurrah! He came home with flowers and a
bottle of rather swanky wine and asked me out.
Oh YAY! YAY! YAY!


## 20 November

Greg has been home on time a lot lately, and he's done a
lot of the cooking. Hurrah! Greg is back! Feel a lot better,
am much happier. Think I have been reading a lot into
things lately.
Have been silly.


## 29 November

*11.35*
Greg went out last night. Came home at a reasonable hour.
However, he felt it necessary to have a shower before he
came to bed. Said it was because he was a bit sweaty from all
the dancing.
Dancing? Greg? Hmm. He never dances. At least not with
me.

Suspicions aroused, and there is a heavy weight in my chest. I'm about to snoop on my husband. Perhaps I shouldn't. Just being paranoid. So what if he had a shower? He was sweaty. He was just showing consideration towards me.

### 11.48
Bollocks was he. Am going to snoop. I'm utterly pissed off at being so gullible.

### 11.55
Probably nothing to worry about though. Probably won't find anything. And where do I start snooping anyway?

### 12.04
His penis probably. Haven't seen *that* for a while. Wonder if I'd recognise it in a line-up? Eugh! There's a horrible thought. Now have an image of a line-up of men hidden behind a wall with little holes cut specially for their dangly bits. One of them is Greg's penis. Don't know who the others belong to. They've just appeared in my little head looking like strangled turkeys.

### 12.30
Silly conclusion to draw just because Greg had a shower before coming to bed. Feel like a bit of a shit for snooping but something is telling me that all is not right. The only way to satisfy myself that nothing is going on is to snoop. So I'm going to do a bit of washing. Will wash Greg's clothes. The ones he wore last night. Sure I won't find anything.

### 13.25
Bastard! Have been staring at Greg's sweatshirt for the past thirty minutes.
It's smeared in lipstick. And smells of perfume. Cheap

slapper perfume. Doesn't necessarily mean anything. Just means he's a lying cheating wanker.

That's all.


*14.17*

Now what do I do?

Do I pick up the sweatshirt and go storming into the study and say 'who the hell have you been fucking?'

No. Bad idea. Would only annoy him. Won't do that.


*15.12*

Picked up sweatshirt and went storming into study. Did not, however, say 'who have you been fucking'. Nope. Said, 'Who the hell have you been shagging and did she do it doggy?'

Much better.

Am a lady after all.

No need for vulgarity.

He gave me a lopsided look, the sort you would give a five-year-old that has just asked if money really does grow on trees, and smiled a patronising smile.

I swear for a split second I wanted to stab him with a pair of tweezers.

He took the sweatshirt from me, smelt it, and told me it wasn't perfume.

No?

It was sweat.

Strangest smelling sweat I've ever smelt.

So, I asked why he had turned it inside out.

He said that that was just the way he had taken it off.

Hmm, so why is there lipstick all over it?

A brief pause – mind working overtime and then, 'I was dancing with Debbie, you remember Debbie?'

I do indeed remember Debbie. It's very hard to forget meeting the world's only human bulldog. He pointed out that she was a bit pissed – bless her – and she was dancing with him and kept trying to reach up for him.

To do what?

'To kiss me.'

Oh that's okay then. Hmm. No it's not, but do go on.

'Well she kept trying to grab me, and as she's only small she lost her balance and went face first into my shoulder. Hence the lipstick stain.'

So there.

Silly me. Why on earth was I suspicious? Darling, loving husband. Such precise and believable excuses.


*18.30*

My arse. Am not stupid. I may be gullible, I may be far too naïve, I may be too trusting. I am not, however, a pushover, or stupid. Or swallowing a load of crap like that.

Seed planted. Tree growing. Have something tangible to act on. Just need a bit more evidence. Then I can act.

I feel strangely alive. What the hell is wrong with me?


And so my marriage began to crumble, and I knew that I could do nothing to save it. If I'm honest, I don't think I ever wanted to save it. There was nothing more left; I had no more feelings, no emotions left. Which was fine by me – emotions are shit.

Emotions are our creator's way of having a laugh, because emotions are beyond our control: we can't make ourselves fall in love, and we certainly can't make ourselves *stay* in love, so sometimes at the most inopportune time and with the most inappropriate person, love makes its way to us, and that's where the danger lies.

Because love is stronger; it transcends time, but it also comes with a whole lot of lust, and though it's a wonderfully electric time, sometimes the two become confused, but they are fundamentally different.

Lust is wonderful, but its initial animal magnetism never lasts. It's over within weeks, perhaps it will last months, but it will die; lust is about the most basic human function: sex.

Love is deeper than lust. With the right person and with the right amount of trust and respect, love can last forever.

Love and lust should go hand in hand along with support, friendship, companionship, and of course the longing that comes with being with a person you feel an affinity with; the longing to be with someone for no other reason than when you are with them, everything seems somehow lighter, easier to handle, life isn't complicated when they are around – love and a whole lot of hard work in between, makes a relationship work. The myth of the perfect hearts and flowers easy relationship just doesn't exist, because women are women and men are men, and never the twain shall meet.

But in the long run, it can work out pretty good, and the bumpy grindy bits are good too.

However, if you don't work at it, and you lose either love, respect or trust, then you lose the relationship – people may stay together out of a misguided sense of loyalty, but resentment will creep in, and the poison will fester, and pretty soon you've got a boil the size of Brazil on your arse instead of a pretty rose garden with amazing topiary that your friends gasp over. Boils can of course be lanced, but does the memory of a poisonous relationship linger and does it ever really work again?

For me, no. For me you never go back, not once trust has gone, because the most important thing in a relationship for me is trust.

So, when the person you marry, the person you have loved and respected, and agreed to support and honour for the rest of your life, dies before your very eyes, you can't control the range of feelings that well up inside. I'm sure the severity of the emotions vary from person to person, but the feelings must surely be the same for everyone: the helplessness, the lack of control, the paralysing anger and finally the fear that makes you breathless. Feelings that had once been so habitual begin to die, which only makes the rage all the more intolerable, because this person you loved and trusted and supported has stolen a precious part of you. They take away your trust and sometimes it never comes back; sometimes you don't want it to come back.

The future you once had disappears and is replaced by a strange and alien world that you have no protection from. The feeling of utter worthlessness is so overpowering at times that it simply takes your breath away.

Why hadn't I read the signs?

How long had I been treated like a fool?

Did my husband and his mistress laugh at me behind my stupid naïve back? Was I the bitch wife from hell, and did he use the line 'My wife doesn't understand me'? Did he talk about me to her? Did he tell her how gullible and trusting I was? Did he tell her that I would swallow any excuse? Did my trusting nature make it easier for him to start the affair, and worse still, continue it? Did I deserve to be treated with such contempt?

Perhaps I did.

If the signs were there and I was too stupid to see them, perhaps I deserved everything that happened to me. Or was it just that I trusted my husband? Was it that I believed everything he said? Why wouldn't I? He was my husband, he would never hurt me. The only thing I ever did wrong was love him. Or so I thought. Perhaps I didn't love him.

Had the feeling of love I had just become habit? Did I really love him? The passion had long gone, in fact had never been there. I didn't ever have a spark with Greg – I didn't even like him when I first met him and avoided him at any cost. But he chased me, and I succumbed and we became great friends – had we confused great friendship with love?

What was I saying? Of course I loved him, otherwise why would this be so painful? These questions and a thousand more played over and over in my head until I thought I would explode.

I did love Greg, but it really wasn't enough. The man I loved had died and I didn't know where I was or what to do.


## 12 December

*18.30*

Greg has just left for his works Christmas 'do'. Partners are not invited – they never are. He said he won't be late, but that probably means see you at three in the morning.

Have wine, chocolate and *Grease* to watch – would much rather have my night than Greg's – nasty horrible 'look at the size of my wonger' affairs.

*23.00*

Despite the problems we have had, I believe very strongly that Greg and I go together like a Rama lama lama lah-blinkey di blinkeh bonk.

But that could just be the wine talking.

*03.46*

He's not home yet. Knew he wouldn't be. Lord knows why he tries to placate me with tales of being home early.

Silly man.

Ah well, as long as he's safe.

*05.03*

Still not home. He hasn't called.

*08.00*
Am now at work. Greg was still not home when I left, and is not answering his mobile.
Am very scared.
And very angry.
What if he's dead?

*09.00*
Will be good thing if he's dead. Believe I will gain oodles of money and lose one dead-beat husband.
So, hurrahs all round.

*13.00*
Have found the cheating little shit.

*14.30*
Am much calmer now and can now write in diary with steady-ish hand. My husband is a dumb liar and he thinks I'm a typical little policeman's wife.
Well I'm not.
I may be trusting, I may be naïve, but I am not a dumb policeman's wife that puts up with the crap that flies around the incestuous buildings that are commonly known as police stations.
Greg didn't come home last night, so I did my homework. Taking the piss is taking the piss and to not come home all night and to not call, is quite simply, not cricket. I don't get cricket anyway.
Stupid game.
And the balls hurt.
So do Greg's. At least they do now.
Hurrah!

I found out that he left the 'do' with a group of people, a high proportion of which were female. The tiny tinkle of bells began to ring in my ears. I discovered that the cheap slappers lived on the other side of the city to Greg and I. I left work and did a little search of the vicinity in my car.

As luck would have it I drove past Greg, who didn't see me. Had he seen me things could have turned out so differently. But he didn't, so I was able to watch as he lied to me and I was caught between anger and despair and I thought my heart would explode. As he stood in the middle of a busy street and told his wife lie after lie, a part of me died. And a part of me was reborn again. I called him and watched as he took his mobile phone out of his pocket. I saw him look at the caller display and then send my call straight to the answer phone.

I wanted to run him over and crush his tiny little penis.

But that would be bad. For me, not for the penis. I don't do jail.

Can you take your own wardrobe into jail? Might do jail if you could do that. Am procrastinating again. I do that when I'm nervous, or angry, or indeed on the verge of a murderous spree. Anyway, I decided to call him again and this time he answered and put on his bemused, 'Shit have just woken up, gosh where am I, ooh didn't I have a lot to drink last night' voice. He didn't realise I was looking directly at him. Dumb assed little shit.

So, I asked him where he was. He said he didn't know. I told him to look at a road sign. He said he was in a flat and couldn't see one. I told him to ask someone. He said there was no one to ask. I told him to ask the man in the blue jacket and black jeans who was about to walk past him.

He put the phone down.

I called him back and told him he was on the Bristol Road, and perhaps he should take up reading as there was a road sign next to him that was clearly indicative of where he was, as road signs generally are. He began to turn round in circles like a dog chasing its tail, scouring the road for me.

I told him, 'No I'm not over there, I'm over here. No, not there. *Here.* That's it! You've got me! *Hi darling, where ya bin?'*

He looked fucked.

And he was.

But not the way I suspected he had been the night before.

He was a little perturbed that I had managed to find him. He will never find out how I did it, but I can be very persuasive and despite my temporary lack of confidence, I am not a fool.

Greg however thought I was.

I loved Greg. I trusted him. Or at least I had. He had pushed a little too far, spent a little too much time away from home, had been a little too grumpy, and far too keen to blame me for everything and so I eventually became suspicious.

Took long enough! How many signs?!

Telling someone they're not interesting, telling someone they're not attractive, telling someone you can't bear to touch them is one thing. It's an extreme form of control. It's takes away one's confidence.

Taking someone for granted, pulling the wool over their eyes and treating them like a fool is just plain stupid. It makes one suspicious. It gives back a little of the stolen confidence. But control freaks are too dumb to see that.

Which is why they get caught.

Except of course, as luck would have it for him, Greg didn't get caught. And he didn't get caught because I still had no proof. And boy did he know it.

He lost his temper and accused me for not trusting him. He told me that I made him feel like a bear in a cage that was being prodded with a stick. Why couldn't I just let him have a night out for Christ's sake? Why did I always have to be so controlling, so demanding? Was it any wonder that he didn't call me? He knew I'd only make him go back into the cage.

And for a split second it almost worked. I almost apologised. I felt sick to my stomach as I realised for the first time that this was how he controlled me. He could take any situation and turn it around and around, until eventually everything became my fault and I would see everything from his point of view and finally I would apologise and he would put his arms around me and tell me that it was okay, he understood, he could live with it, but I had to learn when to back off. I had to understand how difficult I was to live with, but that he loved me, and he could cope with me.

*He could cope with me.*

How many times had I heard that and been thankful that someone could 'cope' with me? How many times had I thanked my lucky stars for Greg and the fact that he could 'put up' with my unreasonable behaviour? How long had I allowed myself to be manipulated like this?

The realisation was like a veil parting before my eyes. I could see everything clearly for the first time, and now I knew. Now I recognised how clever Greg could be and for the first time, *I* was able to manipulate *him*. I played along with his charade and once again I became the perpetrator. I told him I was sorry, that I had just been worried about him, and could he please in future call me if he was going to stay out all night. I squeezed a tiny tear out of my eye, and before long I was in floods of tears. I was crying at the death of my marriage and at my own stupidity, and I felt utterly alone. But Greg didn't know that. He thought I was crying because I had once again upset him, I had crossed the invisible line once more; I had gone too far. Again. And he smiled at me. And he patted my head and kissed my cheek, and he brushed my tears away with soothing words.

We went home and he cooked. And the veil fell to the floor and a new Chloe slowly emerged.

What awaited her was the first in a catalogue of events that would shape her future and lead her along a long path of hopelessness and despair that would turn *my* life upside down.

On 14 December I went Christmas shopping with my mother. There's something about Christmas, with its decorations, it *faux* festive cheeriness, and the families that walk hand in hand that can make you feel warm and fuzzy, or cold and lonely.

I had not been married six months, and I was cold and lonely. My first Christmas as a married woman would also be my last. I knew that something was happening in my life and I had no control over it, and the terror was suffocating.

Walking among the happy couples and the carefree families, as the tinny Christmas music looped in the background, something stirred within me. I didn't want my marriage to be over, yet I knew it was, and nothing would ever retrieve it. I wasn't living any more, I was existing, and there was no joy in either life or love.

But I needed evidence before I could confront my husband, and I knew what I had to do in order to get it, but still I hesitated. In carrying out the act I would be betraying him. Here I was allowing myself to be treated like a doormat, and my only concern was for my husband, and how I was going to have to snoop behind his back.

What can I say? I'm a freak. I trust and am trustworthy, and I don't like to snoop because the very act of snooping is to admit that you don't trust someone. If I snooped, I was crossing another line, and that line would always be crossed: I was admitting to myself that my husband was untrustworthy. The very act would seal my future, but I consoled myself with the fact that perhaps I would find nothing.

Arseholes.

I knew I would find something.

Except *nothing* could have prepared me for what I was about to discover . . .

I hate computers.

Computers stole my marriage. Computers and a man with no control over his dumb stick. And a loose-legged slut. And an online dating agency. And Friends Reunited.

Don't get that website. If you wanted to stay friends with someone you knew at school why didn't you write to them? Or phone? Or visit? Why did you have to wait for a website? Only sad, sad people with something lacking in their lives get excited at the concept of Friends Reunited. That, or people who are a teeny bit insecure and want to say 'Hey look at me, now look at what I do, and check out the size of my pay packet.' Or the man who wanted to have another furtle with the girl in 3G who would have stolen his cherry but he popped a bit too soon, but hey, he's had lots of practice since then and 'the wife' will never find out, so why not hop on board this little lady?

Should be called Furtles Reunited not Friends Reunited.

I couldn't care less what Catherine Silke or Claire Owens are doing. I hope they're happy, but if they're not, why should I care?

I don't.

Sorry.

Anyway this is the downfall, the fallout, the beginning of the end. This is the earthquake.

## 14 December

Went Christmas shopping today.

Couldn't concentrate. Too many happy smiley people pretending to be happy smiley people simply because it's Christmas.

Stupid.

Just be sad and miserable and be done with it.

I did.

And what's with the piped Christmas music anyway? I know Roy Wood and I are personally acquainted but really, I don't want to hear the same sodding song over and over again. Must give Roy a call, it's been ages. In fact it's been twenty-six years. Wonder if he'll remember me? Can't be every day you nearly suffocate a seven-year-old with your arse.

I'm sure he'll remember me.

I can't be bothered to go into detail. I don't want to write the words. Needless to say my husband has been to an online dating agency and touting for 'no strings sex'. He joined at the beginning of November. We had been back from our honeymoon for three months.

I snooped around the computer and discovered his online username and password, and I used them.

He is a wanker of large proportions.

He has been approached by lots of women and has entered into online chats with several of them.

I felt sick when I read his words.

He was very honest bless him, he told the lovely little ladies that he is married, and furthermore, he plans to stay married – lucky me! His wife will never know because his job can cover a number of sins: he can simply say he's working overtime.

Apparently I'll never find out.

His wife sounds like a right dumb cow.

Hang on a minute, I'm his wife! And a dumb cow.

I then read his profile of likes and dislikes. He likes to go out for a nice meal and then perhaps go dancing.

Who does he think he is, Frank Fucking Sinatra? Did Frank ever fuck Sinatra I wonder? Can I write that without getting sued? Course I can. Frank is dead. Bless him and his little Mafia ways.

Anyway, Greg is also 'easy going'. Yes he is. He's very easy going. In fact he's just plain easy. He's also very funny, according to him.

What I find funny is the fact that I've *also* joined this little online dating agency under an assumed name and I'm going to nail his ass and gather as much evidence on him as I can. Now *that's* funny. What's also funny is the fact that Greg thinks he's over six-foot tall. If Danny De Vito is over six foot, then yes, I suppose Greg is. But Danny is as tall as a blade of grass. Can I write *that* without getting sued? My fine and faithful husband is also very 'athletic' (!?) when it comes to sex.

Yup. Have to agree with that one. He loves to run off in the opposite direction. I'm wondering now, given that he's such an athletic lover, if it was all part of foreplay and I was supposed to chase him?

Don't do chasing.

Ah well.

My online user name is Dusky Maiden. I am part Greek, at least online I am. My name is Natalia Charalambous. I'm a computer programmer. A computer programmer that knows bugger all about computers.

I'm a sneaky cow. I'm back in control. I'm on the edge. I'm terrified. I'm worthless. I'm disposable. I can't control my heartbeat. I've been sick. I'm in shock.

I've just called Greg to tell him I know.

He said, 'You know what?'

I said, 'I know you fancy yourself as a bit of a Frank Sinatra and want no strings, adventurous sex while your wife thinks you're at work.'
He put the phone down.
He called back and said he was on his way home.
I'm about to make mince pies.
I am cool, and calm and making mince pies as though there's nothing wrong.
My husband has been unfaithful.
I'm making mince pies.
My marriage is over.
I'm making mince pies.
My future is fading.
I'm making mince fucking pies!


## 15 December

Mince pies are being used as foundation bricks. My marriage is not quite as over as I thought, but it's on the brink. Greg came home and I was very calm. I asked him what he wanted to do.
He looked shocked. He was expecting a knife in the back. I quickly put the knife I was hiding behind my back, back in the drawer. As I've said, I don't do jail, otherwise there would be a corpse on the carpet. I told him we could either talk about the way he had been acting and treating me and he could confess to any 'wrong doing' and we would take it from there.
Or the marriage is over.
The end.
He chose the first option. So I told him to talk to me, to tell me everything, the whys, the whens and the whys again. The whys. The fucking WHYS!!
So he told me. He was afraid. He had no idea marriage

would make him feel so different. So responsible, so trapped.

I pointed out that *nothing* had changed and the bills were still split fifty-fifty and everything was still equal. Oh and by the way I paid for the wedding. So what the fuck?

Didn't handle that last bit too well, but for God's sake, if ever there was a pathetic excuse.

He said he didn't mean trapped in a monetary sense, he just felt so – oh he didn't know.

I said, 'Oh well, that's okay, please do go ahead and stick your penis in the next available vagina and continue to do so until you feel better.'

Actually I didn't say that. I didn't say anything. I just looked at him.

And he cried.

And then I cried.

And he asked me if I could forgive him. I asked if he had anything he wanted to tell me. He said no. I told him I forgave him.

And I thought I meant it.

*05.00*

If I have forgiven my husband, why do I plan to go back onto the website and see if he's still soliciting on there? Why am I still planning on tracking his movements? Why do I plan to approach him under my assumed name and lure him into a meeting?

Perhaps I won't.

I'll see how things go.

Am knackered and have to go into work and entertain an author, and do lunch and pretend everything is fine.

Well, I've had a lot of practice.

Christmas came. It was good. In fact it was a wonderful Christmas, and part of me began believing that Greg and I really had worked through our issues. We were spending time together again, we were laughing the way we used to laugh, and we began talking openly about what upset us and what made us frustrated.

I went back to the online dating agency using his password, only to find that it was no longer accepted. I revisited it using my own password and looked for Greg. I found him, and I wrote to him. He didn't write back.

So, everything appeared to be going swimmingly.

Appearances are shit.

The day after New Year, Natalia Charalambous had a response from PD43.

PD43, it turned out, was Greg. He was sorry he hadn't been in touch with her, but his wife had found out about his online 'shenanigans' – his frivolous little word, not mine. He went on to explain that he had to 'lie low' for a while, because his wife had even discovered his password and username – the sneaky little cow – and he had to change them.

He asked me if I'd had a good Christmas. Did I get what I wanted? Or was there was something extra I wanted that he 'could give me'.

Eugh!

He then told me that he had attached a picture of himself

for me to look at, and would I please be gentle with him, he couldn't take criticism. Which was true. He was pants at being told he was crap. Or ugly.

I opened the attachment and was sick. Right there in the study, straight into the wastepaper basket.

I was staring a picture of my husband on his wedding day. Signing the fucking register. There was a Chloe-shaped hole where I should have been.

This was my husband.
He was soliciting his own wife for sex.

Once I had calmed down I printed the pages, and added them to the other prints I had.

I then called a solicitor. And then three estate agents. And then I called Greg and told him I was leaving.
And I left.
And my world continued to shake . . .


## 3 January

*16.03*
Am back in old bedroom. Back in the bedroom I left behind twelve years ago, when life was going to be an adventure and I would never get married or 'belong' to anyone.
What the fuck went wrong with my plans? Can't understand why I'm so calm about it. My marriage is over. Am very calm. Will get through this no matter how hard it may be. Calm. Calm. Calm.
The future is bright.
Perhaps not orange, but certainly not grey.

*16.27*
Have smashed my favourite wedding picture to smithereens. Don't care about anything. Not even the piece of glass sticking in my foot. Don't care that I'm bleeding all over the

carpet. Nice new carpet that my parents installed after my last stopover. Wonder if they could see this coming, wish they'd told me! Could have saved a fortune.

*22.04*

Is it possible to be with someone for so long that they become nothing more than a custom? Can loving someone fade from passion into habit? And once the passion has gone and the routine begins does that mean that you no longer love, or is it simply a case of the relationship maturing?
What's more important, passion or compatibility?
Does any relationship ever have an equal amount of both?
And where does the love go?
Is it love if you look forward to seeing someone, to know how they like their coffee, to know what films they will or will not watch, to know what position they sleep in, to know what food they like, to know what will put a smile back on their face when they are low? Or is it a slippery slide into boredom and familiarity? What happens to a relationship when love and passion are replaced by love and familiarity? How long is it until familiarity becomes boredom?
Does love really last forever?

*03.07*

Wonder what Greg is doing? Wonder how he is? Hope he's okay. Wonder if he's asleep? Bet he is. He could sleep through a nuclear war. Which is probably a good thing. Perhaps I should have tried harder to understand his moods. Maybe I didn't probe enough.
How much probing does he require for God's sake?

97

## 17 January

Oh hurrah! Am in hospital! In the pigging freaking shitting hospital!

My marriage is over, my life is in disarray and now I'm hooked up to a saline drip being denied food and am human guinea-pig to a bunch of not at all ugly medical students. Life is goooood!

My own fault I suppose. I have never coped very well with stress. My stomach copes even less.

One minute I was at a friend's house, talking about Greg and how confused he must be and how I didn't know how to help for the best and blah, blah, blah . . . the next I was on the floor eating carpet grippers.

I didn't want to alarm my friend, so I pretended that there wasn't a fire raging in my stomach and that I didn't feel light-headed or dizzy or even a tiny bit nauseous.

And so I decided to drive back to my parents.

It wasn't far.

About ten miles.

I was fine!

Except I wasn't. It was gone one o'clock in the morning, and fortunately the roads were rather clear. They were also rather icy. And, being the talented driver I am, I found every ice patch on the road, and did some impressive synchronised spinning. Except there were no other cars on the road so that would make it just plain spinning.

I managed to get home, and called a doctor before once again falling into a dead faint and whacking my head on the hard kitchen floor. When I came round again I thanked God for small mercies – my mother was in bed!

Clearly not a good mother – she didn't hear her daughter's delicate little head crack like an egg on her kitchen floor –

thank goodness. Had she been up there would have been pandemonium, she doesn't cope very well when her children are in pain. In fact she goes to pieces.

Must be a mum thing.

I find it a pain in the arse and not being a mum can't relate *at all* to such emotions.

So, I woke up on the kitchen floor, with a loud ringing in my ears. Took several seconds before I realised that the ringing was actually from the phone, and not in my head. I answered it quickly before the rest of the house awoke.

It was the doctor, telling me there was an ambulance coming for me.

Crikey.

Must be ill or something.

As the doctor spoke I saw a blue flashing light outside. Shiiiiiittttt! My mother! Turn the freaking lights off, she'll wake up!! The doctor told me he had no way of communicating with the ambulance crew and perhaps I should go and open the door.

So I did.

There were two ambulance 'persons' and they both had very loud voices.

'WHAT IS YOUR NAME?'

'Chloe.'

'CAN YOU TELL US WHAT THE DATE IS?'

Yes I could, I'm not Anastasia. I don't have amnesia.

'WHAT'S THE PROBLEM CHLOE?'

I'm not deaf.

'WHAT?'

Don't know. Keep fainting, and I think I may have a perforated eardrum, and if you don't shut up you'll wake my mother and then you'll have a hysterical woman with crazy bed hair to look after as well. So please for the love of God SHUT UP!

Didn't actually say any of that, just screamed it in my head. But it was too late.

Crazy bed hair mum was awake. In fact crazy bed hair mum was up and standing in the hallway in a purple dressing gown watching as two ambulance people poked and prodded her daughter. So she did what any crazy bed hair mum would do. She put the kettle on. She asked if they wanted sugar. She didn't listen to their answers, because crazy bed hair mums don't listen to answers. They just function.

I was asked very loudly if I thought I could be pregnant.

There was a tinkling in the kitchen as the best china hit the floor.

Crazy bed hair mums have the hearing of bats.


## 4 February

My husband has been to see me.

I didn't want him to.

In fact I specifically asked for him *not* to be told. I didn't want him there simply out of a sense of duty. Why don't parents listen to simple requests?

Within a nanosecond of my parents leaving the hospital Greg called the ward sister and asked to speak to me. Told him I was fine and that he didn't have to visit.

He told me to shut up.

Charming.

This separation thing was clearly working.

So, he visited. For at least twenty minutes, and then left. He was rather cagey and looked like shit. Can't say I was pleased to see him, but he was rather nice in an 'I've got to do this as a husband' kind of way. Said he would be there when I have my day of tests.

Said, 'Eh? What tests?'

He left and said the doctors would be talking to me.

Shit. Have got awful illness. So many things I wanted to do. Like learn to swim. And have a marriage.

And now have some horrid disease that will stop me from doing all the simple things in life that only become important when you can't do them any more.

Have awful, awful illness.

Shit.


## 6 February

Hmm. An endosocopy they said. It's just a tiny tube with a camera. A tiny tube with a camera that is inserted into the mouth stuffed down your throat, allowing the doctors to take a look at the stomach.

Nothing to worry about, *they said.*

Okey-dokey I thought, sounds easy enough and besides, Greg was going to be there to hold my hand. I could be a big brave soldier.

So, they wheeled me in and I was unconcerned, just looking around at all the pretty shiny things that probably inflicted untold horror. But not to me. I was having a teeny tiny tube inserted into my mouth, and I probably wouldn't even know it was there. I was one of the lucky ones. Yup. Lucky, lucky me.

Luck my arse.

My suspicions were first aroused when they told me they couldn't numb my throat, and I would therefore be wide awake and would feel everything.

Several people winced. I believe one may have made the sign of the cross.

I was then whisked off into the suite-cum-torture-chamber before I could run away.

There were five people inside the dungeon. I assumed that one of the doctors was a big *Star Wars* fan because he waving around a pretend light sabre that had pretty sparkly things flying out of the end. Didn't think he was very professional playing with his light sabre in front of a patient, but hey-ho, it could have been his coffee break.

They asked me to lie down on the bed and turn my head to the side. Easy peasy. Then a very nice young doctor with very gentle hands began stroking my hair and told me to relax. This was great. Free head massage and relaxation.

I began to relax and became aware that my ankles were also being held. I tried to put all thoughts of kinky sex games out of my head. The *Star Wars* fan with the light sabre came over to speak to me, and as he approached the doctor stroking my hair stopped being nice and held my head in a vice like grip.

Shit.

I'd been kidnapped and thrust into a porn movie. Probably end up dead. Shit. Was about to become the main star of a snuff movie. Definitely end up dead. Or at least very sore.

I began to struggle and tried to release my head from the grip. At that point two more people appeared from nowhere and held my shoulders. So now I was being held by my head, my ankles and my shoulders. And Darth Vader was heading straight for me with his sparkly light sabre.

Except it wasn't a light saber. It was the teeny tiny camera they had mentioned.

Teeny tiny my ass. Oooh! Thank God it wasn't going up *there*!

I have never seen *The Exorcist* but I believe I did a wonderful squirmy Linda Blair impression. There was no way on earth that thing would fit in my tiny delicate mouth. It was like a drain pipe with sparklers sticking out the end.

It went in.

I cried.

Big brave soldier that I am.

I struggled to get off the bed while the drain pipe thing

snaked its way inside me. I was kicking my legs, and I admit a part of me was taking aim. I was trying to push myself off the bed, and I attempted to shake the thing out of my mouth.

Nothing worked.

All the time the man at the head of the bed kept stroking my hair and telling me I was doing really well, that it was almost over, and that I should relax.

Relax.

Yup.

Easy.

There were tears streaming down my face and I was terrified.

And then it was over.

They couldn't see anything.

Which meant more tests.

Pants.

Greg didn't turn up. He didn't call. I didn't see my husband ever again after that. I may have seen a man bearing a striking resemblance to Greg, but I didn't see the man I married ever again.

Life sucks.


## 9 February

*10.05*

Toss features still hasn't called to see how I am. Wanker.

Have been out of hospital for several days now and he hasn't called his wife to see how she is. It's not as though I'm expecting flowers and chocolate, why would I? Didn't sodding well get them before so why would he start now? But a phone call would have been nice. A little teeny call to ask how the tests went. And then I could tell him – freaking awful thanks, but at least you were there to hold my hand. Ooh no. You were missing. You complete arse.

*11.14*
Perhaps he thinks I'm dead.

*11.19*
He'll be out celebrating then.

*12.00*
I am worried about him though. Despite everything, I know that he would call to see if I'm okay, even if he despised me, which I know he doesn't.

*12.33*
Maybe I am a bad wife. Maybe I shouldn't *be* a wife. Maybe. Maybe. Maybe! Life is full of maybes and what ifs and bloody good job too. If we knew what was coming in life, if we could pre-empt all of the situations that make us what we are and shape our future, then maybe we'd still be living in caves.
Don't think I'd do caves. Where would one plug in one's electric blanket?
Aha!
That's it! Maybe I'm too frivolous! Maybe Greg thinks I don't take things seriously enough.
Must try harder.

*12.47*
It's not that I don't care, I do. In fact I probably care too much, it's just that I don't walk around with my heart on my sleeve that's all. Nope.
My heart is shoved right up my ass.
Or so Greg thinks.
Will definitely try harder.

*13.29*
Am going to devise money-saving chart, and show it to Greg and prove to him that I can be sensible and can be grown

up and can take charge. Perhaps I can put a letter in with the chart just reminding him how much I do love him, how much I miss him. And ooh, would he mind just popping his wonger on the table for me to check it for scabs before he pops it anywhere else!

Am a nutter. Do not want Greg. Do not want to be rejected either. What was wrong with me? Should I tell him that there's a hole in my heart? Or that my whole life has been wrenched from me and replaced with an empty cold void? Or that I don't want anyone but him?

Maybe I will, it can't hurt, it might make him feel better.

Hurrah!

Have plan.

## 15.11

Have managed to save almost three hundred pounds a month. Just by cancelling silly memberships and not shopping at over-priced but rather nice stores. Don't *need* to go to a gym; can start running, just as soon as I can do a fast walk without fainting. Also don't need quite as much make-up and clothes as I buy. Am pants at being a married woman. Am pants at being a grown-up. Am simply pants.

Poor Greg. Bless him. He has had to cope with so much.

Except it's *my* money I spend, not his. We split all the bills fifty-fifty and what we each have afterwards is ours.

But it doesn't mean I have to go silly and splurge every month. Not when I know Greg doesn't do that. So I can stop. I don't need retail therapy. Nope. Have no void to fill. Other than the void where my husband should be.

Now I have to start on the letter.

Hmm. Must make sure it's not too wussy and desperate.

## 16.34

Letter finished! Am quite proud of it: not at all wussy and desperate. Shame that I can't keep it, would be good to look back on in years to come and show it to our plethora of grandchildren and say 'This is the letter that saved your grandparents' marriage.'

*16.43*
Silly me. All I have to do is copy the letter into my diary and I can keep it for years.
Plus when the grandkids find the diary after 'I'm gone', they can read about the wonderful love story that was Greg and I. Am most thoughtful grandparent in waiting. So this is the letter:

*Dear Greg,*

*Never in a million years did I think that this would ever be us, and certainly not after just six months of marriage. When did it begin to go wrong? When did you start doubting your feelings? When did it all become too much?*

*I know that it was I that did the leaving, but I still maintain that you are the one that needs the support and understanding of those around you. You have changed so much over these past months that I barely recognise you, but I have faith and a belief that you are still in there. The man I fell in love with still exists, he's just gone on holiday.*

*Some people find that talking helps, and some bottle things up until they almost explode. I know that you are the latter and I have always known that, and as your wife I will be there to support you through times like this, when it all gets too much for you.*

*When you are ready to talk you know that you can always, always talk to me. I am not naïve and I am not a pushover. I know that things have gone very wrong. Any newly-married man that has to spend so much time away from his wife in order to cope, and goes online advertising for 'no strings sex' out of curiosity has a lot of issues to work through, and I*

106

*wonder how far you would have taken your curiosity had I not discovered what you were doing.*

*But I did discover it, and I love you. And with love there has to be trust, one cannot truly exist without the other, they go hand in hand.*

*So I trust you not to hurt me.*

*I trust that when you decide to talk me it will be with honesty and an open heart, no matter what the outcome. I know that you would not purposely hurt me, and I know that you do love me.*

*How long this takes I have no idea. Maybe we will never work it out. Maybe we are destined to go our separate ways and simply be nothing more than a bittersweet memory to one another. Maybe your future wife or girlfriend will hate the memory of me, maybe they will embrace me.*

*Maybe we will be friends.*

*You may move on and be far happier without me. And I without you. But we will always have our memories. And nothing and no one can ever take those away.*

*We are and always will be a part of one another. And I will always remember you, and all that we had, because despite everything, and regardless of events that are beyond our control, you and I loved one another and we laughed together and cried together, and above all we supported one another. And I shall continue to support you until I realise that it is a fruitless effort and that there is no going back. The past is past, and we can only control our future.*

*Through you I have grown, and through you I have changed, and through this I will change again, into who I don't yet know, but the girl that once existed no longer exists. She may have grown up, she may simply have been replaced by another tougher Chloe who has emerged simply to get through this ordeal.*

*Who knows what the future will bring? It may be that this is all happening for me.*

*I know that you don't believe in fate, but I do, and I think that life has a way of guiding us to the right person and the right situation, and the little days of nonsense and heartache vanish when that person appears, or the situation is reached. Maybe there is someone else out there who I am better suited to. Who will love me as much as I will love them, who will share the same outlook as me, who can be supportive and, understanding and, above all, who will respect me.*

*Respect is something that I think you have lost. Where is the respect in going online and soliciting women for sex? You have lost respect not only for me, but also for yourself, and without that you will never move on, and we will never move on. And perhaps there is a woman out there who is better for you. Maybe our time has past. We have grown together and I suspect that we are moving in different directions.*

*Our time together was beautiful and I will cherish it forever, but I will not force you into a situation that you don't want. I will not contact you again, I will not visit our home again, unless it's to collect belongings. I am not fighting for this marriage on my own.*

*A separation means just that. I cannot see you, and I cannot talk to you, until you are willing to be open and honest and discuss things without clouding the issues and apportioning blame when there should be no blame. I need to live my life without you and see what that life is like. A whole new world is opening before me and I will not be afraid of it. I am moving on and I am embracing life once more. And who knows, maybe I will come to the same conclusion as you.*

*That you were a phase. And a beautiful mistake.*

*Life is too short for anger and hatred. Our future is the only thing we can salvage from the wreck of our marriage, and I have salvaged all that I can. The rest is up to you.*

*I love you, and whatever happens I wish you the best, and I want you to be as happy as I know I will be.*

*One day. When I have forgotten how much I loved you.*
*Chloe xx*

Crikey that was good. Don't know where it came from, but I feel rather energised now. And better still, I believe it. I will be okay. One day. YAY for letter writing, so much better than sending text messages.

Have decided not to post the letter. I want Greg to read it when he gets home, and I know he doesn't finish until ten this evening, so I'll take it round to the house while he's at work. Not sure if I want to go into the house though, it will be strange after all this time, walking into the house that was once my home. Still, at least I'll get to see the cats.

Yup! Am taking the letter to the house.

I am.

And I'm going to cuddle the cats.

Miss them.


*17.33*

Am off to deliver letter. When Greg returns from work to a cold empty house that is simply screaming for me and my inane chatter, he will read it and be touched.

I hope.

He might just throw it in the bin. Still, I'll never know if I don't try, so I am definitely taking the letter. Something is telling me to take it and not just post it. Maybe Greg will be in and we'll get talking. Maybe he'll come home early and remember what it was like to have me there after a horrible day at work. Whatever the reason, I know I have to go to the house. Will take diary in case I end up staying and need to write down all the wonderful things that have happened.


*18.15*

No Greg.

It's strange, I feel like an intruder in my own home. The

house feels different, it has no life, it's cold and empty. Perhaps now I've put on the central heating and fires it will feel more homely, and then I'll . . .
PIPPIN!!!

*18.26*
Ah, have had cuddle from little Pippin: gorgeous ginger tom cats can cuddle away anything and they . . .
JASPER!!!

*18.32*
The git ran away from me!

*18.34*
NILES!!!!

*18.43*
Need plasters and antiseptic. Some cats don't like to be cuddled. Some cats struggle and run away when you squish them to your breast.

*18.55*
It's very, very dark. Have only the light from the fires to write by. I'm afraid that if I put the lights on the neighbours will think I'm a burglar and call the police.
Do burglars put the lights on though?
Maybe not.
Will take a chance and put the lights on. It is my home after all.

*19.20*
Have just finished crying. I can't believe that I don't live here any more, I have so many wonderful memories tied up in this house. The new kitchen that I designed. The floor-boards that I sanded and stained. The rooms we were

renovating. The kitchen we spent most of our time cooking and laughing in, the living room where we would sit in front of the fire and eat crap and watch trash TV while a storm raged outside. The garden we were cultivating, the jasmine we planted outside the French windows ready for the early summer months.

The future we had planned.

The hope we had.

The love we shared.

It is all gone.

There is nothing in the house any more, just an echo of what could have been.

I wish I hadn't come, but now I'm here I have to revisit each room. Perhaps it will have a cathartic effect. Perhaps not, I just know that I have to do it.

*20.00*

Life has a funny way of preparing you for the worst. Call it sixth sense. Call it intuition. Call it what you will, life helps out. But sometimes life can't prepare you enough.

There are certain events in our lives that will be forever etched in our memories. Good and bad memories will merge together in a montage of colours and senses that we think have been forgotten, until a certain smell, a certain song or a certain object transports us back through time and we are once again trapped in an event that we thought was only an elusive dream.

Or an all-consuming nightmare.

Today will be one of those days. I will never forget what has happened, I will never forgive. And I will never be the girl I once was.

Today I finally realised what a fool I have been, and how cowardly and self-centred and painfully arrogant my husband is and probably always will be.

Today, I began to live again while simultaneously dying.

111

*20.23*

I went into my bedroom and what I discovered was pants. Actual pants. Of the female thong variety.

Just lying on my dressing table as though they had every right to be there, which of course they would, if they belonged to me, which they didn't.

They are two sizes too big. Obviously belong to some fat-assed slag.

When I saw them I had a moment of utter dumbness while my brain tried to rationalise their existence. I stood staring at them and my mind played an abundance of scenarios that might explain them away. It took only seconds, but for those agonising moments I tried, I really, really tried to salvage something positive, anything, just so I wouldn't have to admit to what was startlingly obvious.

As the realisation slowly dawned and my breathing became more laboured and the pain in the pit of my stomach rose and bought with it the bitter bile of shock, I saw that there was an empty bottle of red wine next to the fat-assed pants.

*My* sodding red wine.

Make that *nine* bottles of red that I have.

I turned away from the dressing table and the evidence that was repeatedly slapping me in the face and looked at the bed.

It was unmade.

Both pillows had indentations on them, the sheets were scrunched and in areas had been pulled away from the mattress, and there were make-up stains on the quilt.

Worse than that, there was a wine glass on my side of the bed, a wine glass with lipstick stains on it. There was another one on Greg's side of the bed.

I have never really understood what is meant when people say that certain things happen in slow motion, but now I do. I turned round and around and surveyed the whole of the bedroom, and slowly, so painfully slowly, more and more incriminating evidence became apparent.

The gold hoop earrings on the tallboy. The miniskirt on the floor. The scrawled note on the dressing table that gave me her name, her telephone number and her address, and that told my husband she had had a wonderful time with him, that the food he had cooked was lovely and that she looked forward to seeing him again on Friday. I stood in the centre of my bedroom as it slowly fell away and my life began to crumble into nothing.

*20.54*

I have been in every room in the house. I don't remember going into the rooms, I just remember being in them, and I remember what I found.

In the bin in the study I discovered photos of Greg and Me, torn into tiny pieces. The dishwasher had two of everything inside. Her shoes were in my spare room, her coat was hanging in my wardrobe, her make-up was in my bathroom along with her facial wipes, and her deodorant and perfume sat in my bathroom cabinet.

My wedding photos had been taken down, my clothes were in black bin-liners.

I have been erased. I am no longer needed and so I have been disposed of.

It's as simple as that. What I can't understand is why. Why do I deserve to be treated like this? Is it something I've done, or am doing? Why didn't he just say he wasn't happy? That he didn't think he could be married to me? Why did he have to lie. Why? Why have an affair? Why the lies, the deceit, the anger, the hatred? Why did he let me believe that I was the one in the wrong? He saw how insane this situation was making me, why couldn't he just tell me the truth? Why did he lie when I asked him if there was another woman? Why? Why am I so calm, so numb?

113

Why do I feel so empty? Why didn't I see the signs? Why is this happening?
Why?
Why?
WHY!!
I will wait for him to come home and then I'll ask him.

*21.09*
No I won't, I'll call him.
Now.

*21.22*
I called him. The conversation didn't go as I thought it would. I thought I would hear his voice and be enraged and scream obscenities at him.
But I didn't.
I asked him when he had taken to cross-dressing. He didn't get it. So I explained and told him that I was at home, and did he mind if I used some of his make-up, and would he like me to put his not so teeny thong in the wash, and oh, what shade of lipstick was it on the wine glass in the bedroom because it looked just fabulous.
He put the phone down.

*21.33*
Do I stay or do I go?
I have been online, and went back to the dating agency website. He is still a member, and he is still soliciting for sex. He has however updated his profile and now claims to be single. Nice. I have printed off all of his recent transactions and conversations that he has kindly kept, and will use them as evidence should I ever need them.
I feel sick.
The slimy persona that claims he is 'sensitive' and 'thought-

ful' and a 'considerate lover' is my husband. And he ain't none of the above.

Shit, my phone is ringing.

*21.40*

It was Greg. Called me a snooping manipulative bitch. Charming.

I asked him to define snooping since I hadn't had to do great deal of searching in order to find the evidence. Told him that if he was going to dip his lollipop into someone else's sherbet then he should cover his tracks more carefully. He put the phone down again.

I can only assume that he is now on his way home. I plan to hit Greg where I know it will hurt him the most. His ego and his pocket.

Am still very, very calm.

Weird.

I have thrown the make-up away – didn't think it would suit me – can't imagine what possessed me to buy such an ugly shade of orange anyway. Have also decided that I don't like using facial wipes, plus I don't recall buying them.

Don't want to waste them though, so will use them as bathroom wipes. Have sprayed bathroom cleaner into them in order to make them stronger – after all, they do have to cut through limescale.

Would be a tragedy if I forgot what I've done and used them as facial wipes, I imagine I would get an awful rash and bits of skin might drop off.

Never mind.

I tipped pepper into the crutch of my enormous thong and finally put a copy of my husband's online activity into the pocket of my nice new jacket that is hanging in my wardrobe. Don't remember buying that either, but it must belong to me, it's in my wardrobe. Am sure that I will think the printout very informative when I find it.

I then left the house that had briefly been my home.
And I have walked towards another life.
A life I don't want.
A life I am terrified of.
A life that will be better than the one I have left behind.
And I still haven't cried.

*00.34*
So! My husband's penis has been on vacation. It has been vacationing in other vaginas.
So! My marriage is over! I am still very calm. Almost liberated.
My husband has been dipping his stick into some slack-assed tart and I'm happy.
Maybe I'm in shock.
I haven't cried yet. I feel in control.
No I don't. I feel as though I'm free-falling without a parachute.
Isn't that what free-falling is anyway?
No it can't be.
Stupid. That would be called suicide.
I'm going shopping.
I'm going on holiday.
I'm going to call Catherine.
I'm going to cry.
I'm going insane.
No I'm not, I'm going to drink.
No I'm not.
I don't know what I'm going to do.
Fuck.

Have spring-cleaned my life and got rid of a wanker.
Hurrah!
Chloe's back!
Actually she's not.

Not the old Chloe.
The old Chloe is dead.
Shit.
Now I'm crying.

Nothing more can be said. My marriage was over, it was time to deal with it and move on. I couldn't divorce Greg until we had been married for a year, so I was anchored to him.

It is said that the most stressful things in life to experience are divorce, moving house, bereavement and losing your job. I ticked every box within the first two months of the New Year. YAY for me and my over achieving ways!

So, in the first month of the New Year, my marriage collapsed; I left my beautiful home and my cats (I know they're just cats, but I loved them!); I discovered that my husband had replaced me with his bit of fluff; and, as if that wasn't enough, I was forced to swallow a light sabre.

Not a good start to the year.

But hey, it couldn't get any worse.

Within a week of returning to work my uncle died, and then I lost my job – no more money in the pot, which is one of the perils of working on Government-funded projects – one day the money is re-routed and Bam! You're out of a job; which meant that I wouldn't be able to buy Greg out of his share of the house, which meant I was homeless, which meant I had to find somewhere to live.

Which meant, as far as I was concerned – and I was, after all, the tragic heroine who had done no wrong – that Greg had not only had his cake but he had eaten it, and taken a slice of my cake as well, and was slowly and deliberately nibbling it in front of me, while I starved. He had everything, I had nothing. Not even a goddamn cat.

But I marched on and within a month I had a new job, I had a new flat, I found myself on the other side of the city living in Harborne and though I didn't know it at the time, it was a move that would alter the course of my life, and I had rediscovered my friendship with Catherine, who not only supported me when I was uncontrollable and beyond pain, but she found me the flat, and got me the job. She was my guardian angel, and I doubt I could ever thank her enough for what she has done. She probably saved my life.

But at times I was numb.

I didn't cry, because I didn't think I wanted to.

But now I know that the emotions were being suppressed until I felt I could cope. To everyone else I *was* coping, and I even believed it myself; I was happier and more confident than I had been for years, so of course I was happy. But there were times when I felt unwanted; I didn't belong; I wasn't good enough. And I felt out of control, everything appeared to be happening *to* me and I was just going along with it. The months merged into one another and soon it was April, and it was a beautiful month, the weather was hot and promised us that summer was not far away: it was the sort of month for sitting outside cafés and doing lunch.

And one fateful day, toward the end of April, that's just what I did . . .


## 29 April

When I was a little girl my bestest friend in the whole wide world was Sophia. She was everything I wasn't. She delighted people with her delicate, blonde petite-ness, while I confounded everyone with my dark wildness. She was called

Princess. I was called Gypsy. The psychological effects go deep. Go figure.

Sophia and I had a friendship that would last forever; it would break barriers and cross oceans. We would never be apart, we vowed that when we grew up we would meet every Saturday afternoon and 'do' lunch, but most of all, we would never ever, ever lose touch.

Haven't seen Sophia for almost five years.

We talk about three times a year on the phone, and after the initial awkwardness that accompanies such infrequent contact, we begin to relax and talk like old friends again until I forget why we lost touch.

Saw Sophia today. Remembered why we lost touch. She is very loud, very opinionated – nothing wrong with that, I have one or two opinions of my own that I occasionally like to share – however, Sophia somehow manages to have an opinion without actually saying what she has an opinion about.

Or why.

Or what her opinion actually is. Sophia just likes to disagree. And she tells you she loves you, and she misses you. And 'My god you look super. Shit Gyps' – she still calls me Gypsy – 'if that's what divorce does for you I'll be getting one myself, you look fabulous. Does wonders for the sex life too I hear, although Rick and I have no problems there, at least not any more. I must tell you about this fabulous little clique we've discovered . . .' And so on.

This is all when she's sober. It gets worse when she's had a glass or three. Sophia is embarrassing. And loud. And she swears a lot.

Sophia is the sort of person you *have* to get along with; because no one has the balls *not* to.

Despite all of this she remains my friend. Because Sophia and I have a bond that goes deeper than superficial conversations. Our friendship is bound not just by compatibility, but by trust, and love. And the memories that go with such a friendship are as precious as the childhood we once shared. Sophia knows things about me that no one else will ever know, as do I about her. And we both know that we will go to our graves carrying those secrets. We are link to a past that has been irrevocably lost and yet remains tantalisingly close. When I am with her, the carefree memories come flooding back and I can almost reach out and touch the image of two little girls as they skip hand in hand.

One has crazy dark curls that tumble wildly about her face and the other has delicate blond tresses that look spun of gold, they laugh together and play together.

They chase butterflies in the sun, and have nothing but a lazy summer full of hope and dreams ahead of them . . .

Despite our differences, Sophia and I will always be friends. She's just a freak, that's all.

We decided to meet at one of the canalside cafés that align a once deprived area of the city that is now a thriving metropolis of cafés, restaurants and loft apartments. It is the sort of area that to just live there you have to know the Queen, or someone else suitably well off. I know Sophia, so I'm allowed to go there.

I was walking along the canal path in the suffocating heat, cursing my lack of sun block, when I heard an affected 'Coo-ee, over here darling' emit from somewhere nearby. A tingle rose from deep within my stomach. It was a combination of excitement and dread. Possibly a bit of hunger thrown in as well – my eating habits have become very erratic lately and I couldn't remember the last time I ate. I lowered my head, took a deep breath, put a smile on my face and then looked for my lifelong friend.

There was a multi-coloured triffid with wavy arms and a purple floppy hat sitting outside one of the restaurant bars. I could only assume that it was Sophia. The closer I got the more ecstatic and manic the triffid got, and its enthusiasm was catching. By the time I reached Sophia a multitude of memories had been and gone and she was once again nothing more than a very good, very close friend with very bad taste in clothes.

I approached her and told her as much. 'What the hell are you wearing? You look like an extra from *Jesus Christ Superstar*.' It may have been five years since I last saw her, but I was still able to insult her without feeling guilty.

She threw her head back and laughed, the purple floppy hat fell off her head and blew into the canal, and a cascade of thick blonde hair fell to her shoulders and swung in unison. The princess would never die. She may be woefully corrupt now, but she would never die. I felt a familiar feeling of inadequacy as I began to blend into the background. It always happened when I was with Sophia. Suddenly I become bland and wallflower-like.

She dazzled me with her perfect white teeth. 'Darling, colour is the new black. Whatever that means, but it's the thing that gets you noticed. You haven't done too badly yourself.'

I was wearing a red dress, with red shoes and a red bag, and compared to Sophia I was practically beige.

Sophia was wearing an orange and green Pucci print skirt, with a pink spaghetti strapped top, a red scarf tied loosely around her neck and of course there was the purple hat that was now on its way to Worcester. And though I was loathe to admit it, she looked fantastic.

She studied me for a second, taking everything in, then she beamed her famous Princess smile as the world put on their sunglasses. 'You've let your hair grow again. Good. Never suited you short. You looked like that girl in the film where she pretends to be a boy. Didn't understand that film. If she wanted sex with a girl why didn't she just do it? If I wanted sex with a girl I would. In fact darling I'm seriously considering it. So is Rick. Not women of course, he's had his fair

122

share of those. No, he's thinking of dabbling with both. What do you think? Have you ever tried it?' Her voice carried on the soft breeze and vibrated into the ears of the many brightly-clad patrons that surrounded us. I squirmed in my seat and placed an order to God.

The ground remained steadfastly closed.

Sophia leaned back in her seat, turned her face toward the bright sun and closed her eyes. I looked at her closely and marvelled at my very strange friend who didn't give a stuff what anyone thought of her.

How I longed to be like her.

In the background a waiter studied us with an expectant look. I looked at him and he walked over to us with a huge grin, a saucy wiggle and, I suspected, a teeny erection. It was clear he had heard our conversation, along with everyone else, and he was waiting for me to answer.

I thought it best to remain silent.

His shadow fell across Sophia and she looked up at him as he admired her.

Never one to miss an opportunity, Sophia leant forward, pushing her ample, and much enhanced, cleavage together. Two shiny mountains appeared from nowhere and Sophia disappeared behind them. The waiter could barely contain himself. I suspect he was very grateful for the little apron he was wearing. We gave him our order and as we did so Sophia pushed forward even more and I swear she nearly popped.

So did the waiter.

He walked away with a not so much a saucy wiggle as a desperate dash to get to the toilet. She watched as he made his escape and then let out a sigh.

'All the same. Every one of them. Show them a decent pair and they'll sell their grandmothers and leave their wives.'

I looked at her and said nothing.

'Shit. Sorry Gyps. I didn't think. Yours are fine, great in fact. Are they still real? They are? Impressive. Well, I'm sure they're not the reason your marriage . . .' She reached over the table and took my hand in hers. 'I really am sorry. But I meant what I said before. You look great. How do you feel? Really.'

I lied, as I have become used to doing.

'I feel fine. In fact I feel great.' While I meant it, I also didn't. I was as confused as a fish. Sophia then asked if I had ever considered being a lesbian. Couldn't say that I had. She told me that ooh darling I must. I didn't know what I was missing. Think I might actually. Would be like having sex with myself. And I already know what that's like. Much better when a boy's involved. Or one of those buzzing things. Not that I've ever used one. Would be far too embarrassed to buy one. She told me I should live a little, and that she was going to 'do it'.

I had been aware for some time that Sophia and Rick didn't have a traditional marriage. I think the phrase 'sexually ambiguous' was invented for both of them. Still, whatever makes you tick. I always think, each to their own. This, however, seemed a little extreme. Plus they had two children. My face obviously betrayed my thoughts.

'Don't look so shocked Gyps. I'm not turning gay or anything. I'm just giving it a whirl.'

'Giving it a whirl? It's a marriage, Soph, not your next Mercedes. How the hell did you come to this decision? What about Lauren and Charles?' They were after all my godchildren, so I thought I should look out for their interests. Before she could answer the waiter returned with our drinks. The saucy wiggle was back, as was a cheeky wink directed, of course, at Sophia. She wasn't interested. 'Sorry darling. Wrong sex.' And she turned her attention back to me.

This only succeeded in making the waiter's grin broaden, and he disappeared.

I suspected a bulk order of tissues would be required on the next stocktake.

I looked around and it became increasingly apparent that our conversation was attracting much attention. Which was hardly surprising given Sophia's inability to be discreet. All of the men had wistful far-away smiles, and all the women looked disgusted, with the exception of one or two, who just looked intrigued and were waiting for the next instalment.

I had no idea how I looked to them. I hoped I didn't look sexually ambiguous. How does one look sexually ambiguous anyway? In an attempt to keep our conversation private I leant forward and whispered, 'Why the sudden change. Why now? Does Rick know?'

'Oh darling he's going to *be there*. It's a new group we're part of. You really must come with us. And the twins will never know. We're not having it at our house. Good Lord no. Think of all the sheets that would need washing. I think it would do you the world of good. Bring you out of yourself.'

The thought of Rick seeing me naked made me shudder. The thought of me seeing Rick naked made me sick. Rick plus naked plus rutting made me suicidal. Rick and I together and naked and rutting was an image that will stay with me forever. I will probably never have sex again.

'No thanks Soph. I don't need to be brought out of myself or anyone else, thanks. What is this group anyway? The local swinging set?'

'My God no. Nothing as simple as that. We've had to wait months to join while our backgrounds were checked. And our bank accounts. They don't just accept anyone, you have to earn a certain amount of money. And you have to pay an annual subscription. And then you have to meet the owner of the club, and if she likes the look of you and thinks you'll fit in, then you're in!'

She told me that the woman who owned the club set it up while she was going through a divorce from her millionaire husband. He was about to leave her destitute and she needed income, and being on the inside as she was, she knew how popular a sex club would be.

So there.

She did it.

It was a huge success and she's now a millionaire in her own right.

YAY for divorce.

'You should come along and meet her. She runs an escort agency as well. Very beautiful girls. You could try that. Earn a bloody fortune. And she only accepts the best so it would be a real boost to your social life.' It was the first time I had ever heard of prostitution boosting one's social standing.

'I'll give it a miss, thanks.' As I spoke Sophia was fishing around in her dainty little bag and produced a business card.

'Here, take this, you never know, you might change your mind.'

I took the card from her. It was plain recycled gold embossed paper, and it told me that Fiona Harp was an entertainment manager for Ambitious Adults.

I bet they were.

The image of Rick rutting came back to me and I quickly stuffed the card into my bag. I'd throw it away when I got home.

The afternoon progressed and soon we had finished two bottles of wine and three margaritas. They had barely touched the side, and though we didn't feel drunk, we were. It was dangerous territory.

She asked me again if I was going to call Fiona. There was a single scene as well. I would fit in there too. Might even bag me a man. Said I didn't need one. Already had one.

She said that she didn't mean the antichrist, she meant a *new* man. Told her I didn't mean the antichrist either. My sex life was fine thanks. Had been having much better and more frequent sex since I'd left him, thank you very much.

Shit.

Had told her too much.

Far, far too much.

She let out a squeal and clapped her hands together, and for the first time that afternoon, she lowered her voice. 'No wonder you look so good. Sex works wonders, doesn't it?'

Actually no it didn't. It was great while it lasted and it was true that it was really rather good, and I may have done a few things that I had never thought possible and I believe one act may have been illegal, but when it was over it was over. An evening of passion preceded a day of sheer loneliness. And a deep feeling of worthlessness.

Somehow I had learnt to switch off. To not care about myself. I was allowing myself to be used and I was in fact also using. There was a deep void within me that couldn't be filled, but for those brief passionate hours I could forget about those empty feelings. I felt alive again. I felt excitement. I felt real. I felt something I had never ever felt with my husband, and it scared the hell out me.

Sophia just sat and listened, not once letting go of my hand. Never before had I admitted this to anyone, not even myself. I had been afraid to put the words onto paper because it would make the situation real. It would make my emotions real.

And that was the most terrifying thing of all.

I had been separated from my husband for three months when I met *him,* and the first time I saw him I felt something so deep and so instant that it terrified me. I was instantly attracted to him. To the point of giggling nerves – and *that* had certainly never happened before. I had never, ever felt such a feeling of connection before, a sense of knowing someone before you've even been introduced, and I had always dismissed the notion, but I had now experienced it first hand, and there was nothing I could do about it. I was

127

afraid and confused and would never in a million years admit my feelings.

But to him, I was probably just sex.

A release.

A nothing. And it was killing me inside. No matter how many times I tried to stay away from him, I couldn't.

'He's your heroin Gyps. He gets you through. He makes you feel alive, while making you feel like shit. Please be careful. You need to look after yourself. Do you know how he feels about you?'

I reiterated that I was nothing more than a release, but she was insistent. How could I know that if I didn't ask him? I had to give him a chance.

I couldn't.

If I face another rejection, I may never recover. That and the fact that he wasn't single, he wasn't married, and he wasn't living with anyone, but he wasn't single. And I was more than aware of the situation that I had got myself into. I had no right to ask anything, or to tell him how I felt. I was no better than the cheap slut who slept with my husband.

I was on a helter-skelter ride of emotions and I couldn't stop myself from spiralling downwards. How the hell had this happened? I was the only one that could control my life and determine my future, but I was incapable of taking action.

I was afraid.

It shouldn't have happened this soon. I was supposed to have a fling and nothing more. A quick rumble in the sheets as an up yours gesture to the antichrist, and that was supposed to be the end.

Except it wasn't.

It had gone much deeper than that. At least for me it had. I knew how I felt, and I was loath to admit it to anyone.

Until now.

Shit, shit, shit!

I'd had far too much alcohol. Revealed far too much, and become a dumb-assed self-indulgent girly-girl. I was *not* stupid, and I *could* control my life. I just had to have my heroin to do it. So, I would still see him. Why shouldn't I? Nothing wrong in being a nothing, so long as the sex was good. After all, he wasn't married. He wasn't even living with anyone. He was just *seeing* someone.

He was the one in the wrong, not me.

I looked forward to spending time with him, I enjoyed our conversations, we shared the same attitudes and outlooks and our sense of humour was the same. He made me feel confident, he listened, he had infinite patience and most of all, he made me feel alive in a way no one else had. It was true, I did feel worthless and disposable at times, but that was my problem, not his. I knew the situation before I got myself into it. He said he couldn't make any promises, and I hadn't asked him to. I never would. He called the shots and I just waited. And waited.

I have always maintained that we are each in control of our own futures, and I maintain that opinion.

I'm just not very good at it.

In fact I'm pants at it.

I'm on a tiny little dinghy that's being carried out to sea, and I can't find the paddles.

But they're there.

Perhaps I'll find them one day.

By the time Sophia and I parted company we had moved onto champagne and made a promise to keep in touch.

'I love you Gyps. You're me, do you understand that? *You* are *me*. And *I* am *you*. We are each other. No. it's better than that. We are *one another*. How many people can say that? I mean *really* say that? How many people do you know who are you? I mean really you? I bet not even you are you at times. But I am. I'm always you Gyps. I'll always be you. Much more than I'm me.'

She was hanging onto my right arm at this point and we were trying to make our way towards the taxi rank. She carried her shoes in her hand and she kept flopping toward the ground. I was hanging onto her left arm and flopping over onto the left-hand side. Together we were perfectly balanced. Only true friends have a pissed walk pre-designed. It worked wonderfully every time, and we never forgot it.

'I love you too Princess. You still are you know. A wonderful princess. Except you don't really act like a princess. Not a fairytale one anyway. Cinderella rode off *with* her prince. Not *on* him. The ending is "they lived happily ever after" not "and they shagged happily ever after". Though I think I prefer your version. No one ever hurts you. They're too goddamned scared to. I wish I could be like you. I want to have guilt-free sex.'

'There's nothing stopping you Gyps. You've got the card.'

We reached the taxi and she stumbled in. Before it drove away she rolled down the window and leant out. We hugged and said we would see each other soon. How about lunch on a Saturday? Every Saturday in fact! We wouldn't leave it so long next time.

And then she was gone. And I knew that perhaps another five years would pass before I saw her again. Perhaps ten years would pass. Perhaps I would *never* see her again.

But the girl with the golden hair would always be a part of me whether I saw her again or not. She was my princess. She was my long lost summer. She was my hope.


## 30 April

*11.15*

Uh-oh. Have been emptying my bag from last night. Found the card that Sophia gave me. The one for sexually ambiguous persons of a certain income. I've put it at the back of the diary. Don't know why. Curiosity perhaps. I'll throw it away later. I have a raging hangover and can barely remember anything that happened yesterday. Probably a good thing.

*15.34*
Uh-oh. Sophia has just called. She's told Fiona all about me. If I want any extra income I only have to call her. She said I should take control of my life again. Be in charge. Don't let him use me any more. I should use men the way they use women. Don't know what the hell she's talking about. Told her I am not going to become a high class hooker! She told me I could earn up to five thousand pounds a night.
Yikes.

*15.36*
Hmmm.

*18.18*
Shit. Remember what Sophia was talking about. I told her about my secret lover. My God that sounds sleazy.
Shit.
Hope I didn't tell her who it was. Not that she knows him. Not that I do for that matter. How weird that I'm having regular sex with someone I don't know; I know what his favourite sexual position is, I know the little intimate noises he makes when he's aroused, and yet I know nothing about *him*. Weird, and desperately sad.
Am nothing more than a quick shag.

*19.07*
Have had call from Catherine. She wants to go out. Have decided to go. This hangover is almost over so I might as well start work on another.

*03.17*
Shiiiiiiiiiiiiiit!!!!!!!!!!!
Shitty, shitsters!
Naked man in my bed! Naked man that I think I might be falling a teeny bit in love with. Naked man with girlfriend, that I'm falling a teeny bit in love with is in my bed – am not allowed to be in love. It's against the rules. Fugger.
Naked man that can make me squeak is asleep in my bed. Wish naked man liked me. Am a drunken slut. Am stupid worthless slut. When will I ever learn? Am going to go cold turkey. Am on the wagon. Am not sleeping with naked man again. Ever. Never, ever again. Nope. He could hurt me without ever knowing it. I like him, and I don't want him to not be in my life. That does not make any sense. I can admire him from afar. We can be friends.
Yup!
Am on the wagon. Will fall out of love.
Easy.


**1 May**


*15.30*
Naked man has gone home now. He stayed all morning. We had breakfast. Then he left. Fell off the wagon. Fell off it three times.
Shit.
Am not in control any longer. It appears I'm like a man. Am ruled by an imaginary penis. Except my penis is in the shape of a heart and it beats inside me. I'm heading for a fall. Have set myself up for a fall.
Feel stupid. I'm reading things into situations that aren't there. Every time he calls I fool myself that he really does like me, that it's not just the sex he's after, that he enjoys spending time with me.

132

And then it's the morning after and he leaves.
And I feel worthless and empty and disposable again.
And it's all my own fault.

*17.04*
Uh-oh! I've stumbled upon a horoscope website and have become addicted. I have become one of those tragic people that can't function without the aid of a mystic guide.
Must wean myself off it.
However, it did say that today would be full of ups and downs, and that I would be pleasantly surprised by events. Certainly had some ups and downs this morning. And they were definitely pleasant ups and downs. And ins and outs. Might be some truth in these horoscopes. Have saved it in favourites.
Just in case.

*21.13*
More ups and downs. This time of the emotional kind. Have just finished crying, feel empty, and lonely and pointless. I have no direction. I don't know where I'm going, or where I belong. I don't understand why this is happening. I'm not a bad person. All I did was love Greg and try to make him happy.
But that wasn't enough.
He needed more, he needed someone else. I wasn't enough for him. Or anyone.
Why am I such a pushover?
When did I become a nobody?

*23.09*
I will get through this.
Somehow.
As soon as I stop snivelling.

*23.14*
That card has just fallen out of the diary. The one for
sexually ambiguous adults. Or perhaps for a woman in
control. Aha! Maybe that's how I can take control of my life
again.

*23.20*
Yeah. That's it. That's how people take control of their lives,
Chloe.
They become prostitutes.
Silly cow.

*00.03*
The money's good though.


**2 May**

Am not a slut. Am not a silly cow. I am a woman that has
been liberated from the shackles of a sham marriage and I
am rediscovering my sexuality.
Ohh look – there it is.
Can stop now. Except I can't stop. I don't know how to. I
enjoy it, and then I hate it. Am as confused as a fish again. I
have spoken to Catherine about it – I decided to tell her
about my new-found sluttishness – and she says that it's
clearly done me the world of good. She says I have a new-
found confidence, which I do, but I wonder how much of it
is a shield for how I really feel?
I don't feel I can truly be myself. I can't tell anyone how
lonely and confused I still am. I can't explain how the pain
can be all-consuming, so much so it makes me physically
sick. People don't want to hear about the pain any more;
after all, it's been months and I should be over him.
But it's not Greg I need to get over, it's the deceit.

134

The lies.

The lost trust.

I need to believe in myself again – how do I do that?

I need to understand why he did it, why he lied, and yet I never will.

I need to feel self-worth again, just a small amount will do – just enough to help me like myself again. Enough to want to keep on going.

I wonder how many people actually like me for who I am? And how many like me for *what* I am? Will I ever be good enough simply for being Chloe Richards? The girl that wanted a simple life. The girl that only wanted to love and be loved.

An impossible dream.

*19.30*

Keep looking at the card and thinking, 'Why not?'

Why not indeed.

I mean, how different is it to going out with someone and sleeping with them for nothing and getting nothing but an empty feeling in return? At least this way I'd be making oodles of money.

Not that I really need to, but it's me taking control again. It's my way of saying, 'No, you're not taking advantage of me, I'm taking advantage of *you.*'

Ha! That'll show them. Would have to keep it secret though. My God if my mother ever found out! I would have several feline brothers and sisters. Ahh. Love cats.

Hurrah!

Could move somewhere and have a cat if I became a prostitute.

That would make me feel better.

Yup!

Must become a prostitute in order to have a cat. That's a good enough reason.

Silly cow.

I'll just go out and shag an MP. Then blackmail him. Is blackmail illegal? Don't do jail.

Hang on.

Think prostitution might be illegal.


*22.00*

Have called local helpful police station. Prostitution is indeed illegal.

Pants.

Nice lady gave me the number for the local Samaritans and a mobile STD clinic.

Cheek!

I'm a good girl I am. Have drunk a bottle of Frascati that I bought back from my honeymoon.

For some reason I couldn't bring myself to open it until now. It seems to me that the time to open a bottle of cursed Frascati is when one is seriously considering prostitution as a career move. Goodness! The crap one can write when one is pissed.

Prostitution my arse. Ha! Oh, the things that amuse you when you're pissed.

Am not going to become a prostitute. Silly stupid me.


**5 May**

Wonderful sunny day! Hot, hot, hot! I so do hot! 'Tis the sort of day that fills you with optimism and banishes all wild and unruly thoughts of hookering from one's mind.

Silly thought anyway really. I mean, I'm hardly bendy, and I'm sure you have to be a bit of an acrobat in order to be paid thousands of pounds for sex. Then again, it *is* me. Any man should be honoured!

Not that Greg was.

Pah! His problem not mine. Have a wonderful day ahead of me. Am going for lunch with Catherine. Catherine is excellent at doing lunch. She could in fact give lessons in how to do lunch, she knows the best places to go and is superb company. She and I are very similar. Except I don't think she'd entertain any thoughts of being a hooker.

Then this evening Cath and I are going out for a drink or ten, with friends. Naked man is also going – though suspect he will be wearing clothes. Am going to drink water this afternoon. Am going to drink juice this evening.

Am a new woman.

My body is a temple, not a trash can, or a toxic dumping site.

Feel very positive today. In fact I feel almost high.

Things can only get better.

Have decided to take my diary out with me from now on. The thought of the flat being broken into and this diary being discovered fills me with dread, it all goes back to the mother and kittens scenario. I am pushing all thoughts of being squished by a bus and a paramedic finding the diary, out of my mind.

Glorious, glorious day. The sort of day to plan your future.

Hurrah!


## 6 May

Naked man in my bed. Again.

Clearly need to take the wagon into the garage and get it fixed. Its seats are too darned slippery.

I don't remember anything. What the freaking hell is he doing in my bed? I remember him coming back with me and me making some half-assed attempt to stop this charade. Then I opened a bottle of wine.

Then I got pissed.
Shit.

*11.34*

Uh-oh! Bed just creaked. Shit! Think he's awake. Damn.
Must hide. Stupid. Can't hide, it's my flat. Damn. Toilet has
flushed. Toilet just flushed again. And again.
Damn! Think toilet is broken. Eugh! Hope he flushed his
bits away.
Crikey.
Can hear him getting back into bed.
Cheeky.
Quite like cheeky.
I do cheeky!

*11.57*

NO I DON'T!
This shouldn't have happened.
Bed is making creaking noises, why would the bed be
making creaking noises?
EUGH!
Hope he has tissues.
Shit.
Now what do I do? Must get this man out of my flat. We
must both forget this happened. Must pretend. Must remain
friends. Must not be doing this.
Must be mad.

*12.12*

Am mad. And a slut. Will have shower, hopefully he'll be
gone when I get out.

*12.35*

Have had shower.
Am naked.

Clothes are in my bedroom.

Not going in there.

I know he's still in there; I took a peek through the door.

I'm trapped in my own flat by a naked man in my bed.

Perhaps if I make coffee he'll . . . shit!

He just called me. Now what do I do?

I'll ignore it. I'll just potter around the kitchen, completely naked, making loud noises, and pretend I can't hear him. Except I have nothing to make noises with.

Will sing.

That should get rid of him.

*13.13*

Crikey! He just came into the kitchen and did something rather pleasurable.

Hmm.

Might go back to bed for a bit. Keep him company. Would be rude to leave him on his own, I am the hostess after all, and we hostesses must take care of our guests. Think I may have served over and above my duty as a hostess, but what the hell, I'm a giving kind of person. Very giving.

Oh what the hell.

I'm a grown woman. I can handle this situation. So what if I know him? Might cause a few problems though, after all we do know each other.

Chloe Richards get a grip. You are not going into the bedroom just because the naked man in there can make you squeal. Actually, I am.

And I'm gonna squeal like a pig.

*16.00*

Squealed. He left. Am alone. And feel dirty and worthless. What the freak am I doing? Why did I do that? Didn't realise I could squeal. Wonder if we'll be doing it again?

NO!

139

Remember Chloe Richards. You are nothing. You are disposable. You are good for a laugh and that's it. Stop reaching for the moon.
Am going to hibernate.

*18.00*
Have not been out. Afraid I might bump into him, or anyone else.
Who else knows?
Phone is switched off and I'm not going to answer the door.
Should anyone visit me.


**8 May**

No one called.
No one visited.
I feel trapped and lonely and I want to run away, and I want to belong and I want to feel worthy again. I want to escape the person I was, the person not worth loving, but I don't know who to be. Why do I feel so trapped? I have all the freedom in the world, I can go where I want, when I want for as long as I want, so why am I so paralysed?
I'm pathetic.
I am a slut.
Am empty worthless slut. Why am I unable to get through this? It was so easy at first. I shouldn't have slept with naked man that makes me squeal; I know it's nothing more than a sex thing but maybe I'm not strong enough to cope. It's great while it's happening; it's just afterwards that's a bit crap. Why can't I control my life?
Maybe I can . . .

*12.30*
The pain is sometimes so consuming that it chokes me. I can do nothing but curl up into a ball and cry, and cry.
And cry some more.
Then I feel stupid. It feels as though something is about to happen to me that I again have no control over, and all I can do is wait.
I can't wait. I want to be happy again. I want to belong, I want to love again.
Pants.
I feel so empty. Nothing I do is right, I'm just moving from one stupid situation to another, and I can't control anything.

The hookering card is in my hand. I can think of no reason not to call. I do it for free anyway, why not get paid lots of money? Why not?
Don't think I could do it. I'm Chloe, not Sophia. How do I become more like Sophia?
Maybe it's the clothes. Will go and buy lots of loud scant clothes.
Then I'll call Fiona.
I will.
Will have a glass of wine first.


**10 May**

*06.09*
Can't sleep.
Didn't call Fiona.
Stupid thought.
I can't stop thinking about what I did the other night. How could I have let it happen? It wouldn't have been so bad had it been a stranger that I could forget about, but this was someone I know. And like. And I know that I'm just not

141

worthy enough. Oh crap, just admit it Richards, you're having one of those days, one of those awful days where everything is wrong. The sun is too strong. The birds are too loud, the children too boisterous. Life is too long. I'll snap out of I know I will, I just have to ride it out.

*09.00*

Am alone. The one thing that no one can ever prepare you for is the feeling of utter rejection that accompanies separation. Rejection is rejection, and knowing that all you ever did was love someone and then have that love thrown back at you can lead to nothing but utter despair.

There are times when I am surrounded by people and yet still feel desperately lonely, and worthless. And just plain sodding desperate; desperate for validation, I want to know I'm good enough again. I seem to always be waiting for my next rejection.

And then the moment passes and I am Chloe again. Almost.

*17.34*

The day hasn't got any better. I haven't left the flat; I haven't done anything but sit and think. Thinking is a bad thing to do.

Leads to negative thoughts.

*17.37*

I wonder if anyone knows me any more. I don't think I know myself. I seem to be a hundred different things in one day for so many people yet I don't know which one is me. I can't find Chloe.

See! Too much thinking!

*18.13*

Have figured it out! I know what's wrong with me. The world is full of round holes and I am a square peg! YAY! I don't fit. However, I'm a very flexible peg. Sometimes I fit, but eventually I'll spring out of place, and bounce around until the next hole appears, and for a while, I will once again belong.

I wish people could see me when they look at me. If only I could allow people to *see* me.

On the surface I have a wonderful life. But I would give it all up in a heartbeat, if it meant I could belong again.

There's that word again.

Belong.

I wonder what I mean? I wonder why I don't feel I belong; after all, it's no one's problem but mine.


## 13 May

I haven't seen anyone for a few days. I'm caught up in a world of regret and lust. I have told Cath about naked man and how I feel; she thinks it will be good for me to tell him how *I* feel. And then stop doing it, because it's clearly not doing me any good. She also thinks it would be good for him to know.

Can't see how.

I curled up into a ball again today and cried.

And cried.

And cried.

I can't go through this alone, but I have to. There are times when people ask me how I am, and for a moment I consider telling them the truth.

Lonely.

Worthless

Empty.

Confused.

Cast adrift.

I try to tell them, but I can't; I know that if I tell them the truth they will point out the obvious: I have a better life; a new flat; a new circle of friends. I'm in a much better place than I was, and I should be grateful for that.

It's easier for me to pretend. So I put on the smile, fluff my hair, draw a veil of vivaciousness over the hopelessness and become the Chloe people love and want.

The person I want to be.

The person I *used* to be.

## 15 May

After several days of feeling low I now feel fine again. It seems that a crushing low is always to be followed by a soaring high. I'll have to learn to ride them out, to not think that life is over when I'm feeling low and to not pin all my hopes on the highs.

As boring as I sound, I long for a flat line. For balance. For anything normal. Wish I was normal. People say I'm not normal, and I'm not. What normal person considers prostitution as a viable career option?

Me! That's who!

Stupid thought anyway.

Going out this evening for a meal with friends. Am on the wagon. Am not having dirty empty sex afterwards.

Am not. Am not.

*10.35*
Well, I might.

*10.37*
Nooo!! I'm not going to. Am in charge of my destiny, I am in charge of the chariot.

Or wagon.

I am *not* falling off it.
Even if I do feel a bit frisky.

*18.17*
I am a liberated woman in charge of my life, so why
shouldn't I have hot sex when I want? Might want to do it
later. And if I want then I shall.
Fugger. I'm late. Table booked for seven-thirty. Meeting
Cath at six-thirty. Have ten minutes. Still have hot oil pack
on my hair, and my toes are wedged between pretty pink toe
separators. The left foot looks rather pretty in 'Daring Red',
the right foot now looks as though Frankenstein has taken a
diploma in foot amputation. Can't remember if I soaked my
contact lenses in the rinse solution. Silly thought to have,
I've never ever forgotten, so I'm sure I did it. Bizarre
thought.
Anyway, even if I didn't I have a spare pair, so if all else fails,
I'll stick those in.
Why am I writing in this diary when I am late?
Must call Cath and tell her I'm running a teeny bit late.
She'll know that means desperately late.
Late, late, late.

*18.45*
Am blind. Contact lenses not soaked. Un-soaked contact
lenses put directly into eyes. Would have been less painful
to slit my eyeballs and squirt bleach into sockets. It takes a
while to register the fact that sulphuric acid has been
applied directly to your eyes, so I stuck the other one in. As
soon as the second one went in, the first one started to burn
like hell. Unfortunately, eyes are clever little buggers with a
mind of their own. They screw up into tiny little balls when
they're in pain and you can't prize them open for love or
money. Did a funny little naked jig around the bathroom
trying desperately to get my eyes to open. Jigged face first

145

into the open closet. The pain from my face surpassed the pain in my eyes and I was able to get the contact lenses out. Now all I have to do is stop my nose from bleeding and for my eyes to return to their normal colour: I like the colour red, but I'm not sure it's a very fetching eye colour.

Have called Cath to tell her I'll be even later and why.

She didn't believe me.

*19.26*

Not sure if I should go.

My eyes are still red, I can't put my contact lenses in and my hair looks like an oil slick. Am never, ever, using one of those hot oil thingies ever again, but then I did leave it on for an hour longer than recommended, that might not have helped.

And of course I still have Frankenstein's foot. I look like the Terminator in drag.

Stuff it, I'm going. Just hope I can *see* everyone. Don't think having sex is really an issue.

Unless of course naked man has a thing for Arnie on a bad day.

**16 May**

Darn that slippery greased-up wagon. Fell off it again.

It appears naked man *does* have a thing for red-eyed, club-footed monsters with swollen noses. Either that or it's the free sex.

I started off very strong and aloof and 'we're just friends'. There was no hint or betrayal of our secret liaisons. Then I got a bit tiddly; I *had* to drink to numb the throbbing pain in my nose.

I told him I was tiddly and as such he could take advantage of me as was his want.

146

So he did.
Hurrah!

Except it's not hurrah, not now. Not after the fact. It's most definitely hurrah-infinity during, which is why I keep slipping off the darn wagon. It's as confusing as hell once the door closes behind him and opens on my emotions.
Ah well. We are each in charge of our destiny. I will not slip off the wagon again.
Ever, ever, ever.
... maybe once more, but then that really is it. After all, I am worth more than just a quick fumble.
Except it's not quick. Nor is it a fumble. In fact, it's really rather ... stop it Richards! Get a grip of your life.
It will *not* happen again.
I am most definitely back on the wagon. In fact I am on the wagon, holding the reins and am in full charge. The wagon will not gallop out of control. I am worth more. I deserve more.
I think.
Yes I do.
Course I do.
He is good though.


## 25 May

Well I haven't written in here for a while because I couldn't be arsed. Why would I want to look back on this diary in a few years' time and depress myself? I am trying desperately to gain control of my life, and I will.
I did sleep with naked man again, but I think I'm becoming a little too 'keen'. I can't pretend that I don't care any more. Wish I could do sex the man way: fart; get dressed; go to pub; forget about the sex thing that just occurred. Instead I:

147

have wee that I have been secretly wanting for about four hours and marvel at how flat it makes my stomach; cry; feel shit; dwell for seven days on the sex thing that shouldn't have occurred.

So am on the wagon and am in control; it seems that I am giving away my sexuality and emotions, and I need to switch off. If I can give myself away so freely to someone who doesn't care, then why not do it and get paid?

Why not?

It's no different.

The only difference is I'll be paid money; very good money for sex.


## 26 May

If I do go ahead and call Fiona I will have to stop seeing naked man; which is a shame, because as well as being darn good, he is also darn good company. Men shouldn't be good at both, it's far too dangerous, and very unfair.

It just wouldn't be right, other men paying while he gets it for free. Think it might offend him if I ask for cash up front. So I'll stop seeing him.

I'll do the cold turkey thing and I'll stop going out with the group for a few weeks.


## 28 May

*13.00*

I called her. I've called Fiona, I have a meeting with her next week. I am about to become a prostitute, and I feel fine.

I feel more in control.

I feel . . . relief.
How bizarre.

*15.30*
Shit! What if she rejects me?

# 1 June

*12.00*
I'm still going ahead with it, still meeting Fiona. I've been waiting for the shock to hit me, or the ridiculousness of my actions to slap me across the face, but the more I think about it, the more I can reason my decision.
I will be in control again.
I will not be taken advantage of.
Two days to go . . .

# 3 June

Had my first meeting with Fiona. I didn't want to look like an albino Eskimo for the meeting, so I decided to use some fake tan. I'd never used fake tan before; still, how difficult could it be? Why bother with the instructions?
Because you end up looking like Michael Jackson that's why.
I didn't exfoliate.
Big mistake.
I did use moisturiser though, and then slapped the fake tan straight on.
Another big mistake.
I look like a brown cow with bad skin disease.
How was I to know that if you put fake tan directly on top of moisturiser the body sucks it up at different rates and therefore makes you look a bit . . . patchy?

149

I've usually had three holidays by now and am usually a toasty brown colour, so I don't generally *need* fake tan. My knees, elbows, chin, eyebrows and hairline went a rather fetching shade of brick orange. My top lip looked as though I'd been sucking a cola ice lolly for too long, and I had a tide mark of fake tan around my neck.

Still when I saw the results I didn't panic. I covered up from head to foot, put a scarf around my hair (and hairline) and headed for the shops. I heard that Leichner make-up works wonders, and it's a wow with the theatre crowd – I know, I have friends in the theatre and they told me. What they didn't tell me is that it's very greasy. So I slapped it all over my face and blended the colours in so I looked almost human. The results were pretty impressive.

All I had to do then was dress.

There was no way I could cover my knees and elbows in make-up, so I decided on a white linen trouser suit. Long sleeves, long legs, but nice and cool. Perfect.

A sane person may have thought 'White linen and fake tan – perhaps not'.

Not me.

I was running almost half an hour late, there was no time for sane thoughts. I made a dash for the door and got into my car. It was almost seventy degrees outside and the car was like an oven. The seats had almost melted and the steering wheel was nothing more than a burnt-out Catherine wheel; it was *sodding* hot.

I began to sweat. No, sorry, nice middle-class girls on their way to join a hooking agency don't sweat, we *perspire*. Bucket loads. I was perspiring like a pig. And my face felt horribly itchy. And the backs of my knees, my feet and my arse began to feel very damp.

Great.

If I ran a dating agency I'd have snapped me up. I'm sure there's a niche in the market for a melanin-challenged cow that sweats like a pig and thinks it's a great idea to wear linen and Leichner make-up on a hot summer day.

By the time I got to Fiona's house, the smart trouser suit was nothing more than a creased smelly suit with what looked like poop patches on the arse. When I aim to impress, I go all out.

I was buzzed in through the entrance and followed the sweep of the drive until it reached the front of the house. It was a wonderful art deco house with a separate gym and indoor pool. I got out of the car not at all sure where I was supposed to go, and heard someone 'yoo hoo' me. I followed the voice to the side of the house where the pool was and saw a woman lounging in a swimsuit and large floppy hat. Must be Fiona. She waved me over and the closer I got the more over-dressed I felt. Her swimming costume did little to hide the fact that she was a fan of cosmetic surgery and proud of it.

I didn't know where to look.

She tottered over to me and kissed me on both cheeks. I really felt out of place. I don't do continental kissing, especially when it's just air sucking; still I went along with it and tried to ignore the pounding of my heart.

I declined the offer of a drink and sat precariously on the edge of a sun lounger. I kept telling myself that in a few hours I would be back at my flat and it would all be over.

Except it wouldn't be over, this was just the first step in long and winding road.

Fiona sat back down, took a deep drink of her iced coffee – at least that's what it looked like – and removed her very large sunglasses.

She was really rather stunning beneath the make-up and botox, but she looked older than I suspected she was. I became aware that she was appraising me as much as I was her.

151

'Well, you passed the first two tests that's for sure,' she informed me.

Tests? What tests? I hate tests. I don't do tests.

She must have read the horror on my face and went on to explain. 'I've done a little background check on you, and you passed that. Almost flawless stock. Almost.'

Now I really did feel like a cow in a cattle market. I asked what the second test was.

She told me she liked the natural look, and so did her 'gentlemen clients'. She liked the fact that I had no make-up on, but I should really use sun block on my eyebrows and top lip.

Thank God the make-up had slid straight off!

She then asked me what I thought it would be like having sex with men for money.

I didn't think answering 'a hole's a hole, and you may as well get paid for offering it up. That way, when you're left feeling empty and worthless, at least you have money to show for it' would really help, so I just said it would be like any other business transaction.

For an on the spot answer it went down rather well. Amazing how you can project one image while you're feeling a completely different one, another talent I believe will work wonders in my new profession.

After several hours of questioning and grilling and rules and regulations, I was allowed to leave. Complete with personal mobile phone, 'For the exclusive use of me and your gentlemen, Chloe. No one else must have the number.'

All I have to do now is pass a medical test.

Just waiting for the results now . . .

Easy.

Today was the most surreal day of my entire life. This doesn't feel like my life anymore. I've run away from my life, and the pain and the heartache, and I've become a new

152

person. I'm a new woman now. I'll be in control from now on.
Beyond pain.
Beyond hurt.
I don't need to be loved; I have no desire to be rescued. I don't.
I don't . . .
. . . I don't.


## 7 June

I passed the medical test.
Phew.
Now all I have to do is wait for the phone to ring.
Fugger.


## 13 June

*10.00*
The mobile phone goes everywhere with me.
I don't want it to ring.
But then if it doesn't, does that mean no one wants me?
What's wrong with me?
Stupid idea anyway.
Escort my arse.

*14.35*
Looked up 'call girl' on the internet.
Bad idea.
Perverts.
Then looked up the 'high-class hooker'.
Bad idea.
Weirdos.

*14.52*

Curiosity got the better of me. I looked up 'call girl' + 'hooker' + 'escort'. Oops.

Apparently I need the flexibility of a gymnast and the imagination of a priest. Unfortunately I am as flexible as an iron and have the imagination of a fish.

Thank God for search engines.

I wonder how kinky the men are that pay oodles of money for sex?

Stupid question.

Those men put the 'ink' into kinky. And on their wotsits. Probably. *And* I bet they then try and write with their wotsits as well! Oh hurrah! I do have an imagination after all. Hope to God I don't have to use that one though.


*17.07*

The mobile phone just rang. I panicked and threw it into my underwear drawer and then ignored it till it stopped ringing.


*17.13*

Shit. My knickers are ringing.


*17.47*

It was Fiona. My services are required. Tomorrow.

Shit.

Feel sick.

Who the hell am I? Why am I doing this? Why am I doing any number of things? Why do any of us?

She said he was a regular. Very nice man. She told him I was new and that he was my first. He's going to be gentle with me.

Great!

So now he knows I'm a virgin, as such. He can come up with

many weird and wonderful positions and tell me that it's the norm.
Pants, pants, pants!

*17.58*
I am *not* having sex with a goat.

*18.05*
Or a chicken.

*18.25*
Or any other animal in fact.

*18.31*
Or a woman

*18.54*
Maybe if she was pretty.

*19.08*
No!

*19.29*
Well, perhaps if I was drunk.
I'm drunk now.

*23.42*
Crap.
My toilet's broken.

*00.15*
Tried to fix the toilet.
Oops.

## 14 June

*09.00*
I had a misaligned ballcock.
I'm so scared I can't eat.
Or sleep.
I am, however, making good use of my newly aligned ballcock.
Crap.
My first gentleman is tonight.
Not client. Not customer. Always 'gentlemen'.
Fiona told me in her clipped, purse-lipped manner that, 'We must always refer to them as "gentlemen" because we only *accept* gentlemen, Chloe.'
The rough translation of this is 'if they can pay this much money for one lousy dinner then we'll call them what the hell they like. As long as they pass the means test.'
I had no idea that 'companion procuring' (*not* escorting – 'this is not Essex Chloe') could be so complex. It isn't simply a case of 'Thanks ever so for the dinner, now, do you want the knickers on or off?'
Oh no. It goes far, far beyond that. Firstly there was the vetting of me – you never think you have an STD unless of course you're waiting for the results of several tests, at which point everything south of the navel begins to itch. But it doesn't stop there, the vetting of the 'accompanying personnel' AKA escort, AKA tart, AKA me, is just the first stage.
To be a suitable 'companion procurer' – AKA posh kerb-crawler – you have to supply a clean medical certificate every three months, that is if you're a regular. If you're a mere dabbler, you have to supply a clean medical certificate every time. So keep it in the car. Once that has been done the procurer is then means tested. Six figures and above only. For a simple dinner they pay no less than £2,000.

Which is very worrying. If it's that difficult to become a client – stuff what I'm supposed to call them – then what the hell must they expect in return? To pay that amount of money they probably expect an acrobatic, double-jointed, deeper than Linda Lovelace porn star.

Instead they get me.

Ah well, where there's money there isn't necessarily a kinky sex drive.

Except of course I've read the *Sun*. Or at least glanced at the front page while leafing through a glossy magazine, and it seems to me that the higher the pay packet the more perverse the penis. I read somewhere once that some men put sandpaper inside a toilet roll and then use it to . . .

Think I should stop by the hardware store just in case.

## 10.37

Of course, he may not want any 'extras'. He might just want my company. But what do I talk about? Fiona said I have to take my lead from him, but what if he doesn't say anything? I could tell him about my last facial. That was rather nice. Very relaxing.

## 11.35

They're not called 'extras' anyway.

They're called 'enhancements', or at least that's how I'm to refer to them. If he doesn't mention anything 'extra' at the end of the evening, but I really don't mind the idea of an extra one and a half grand, then I am to say, 'Thank you for a lovely evening. Now, is there any way I can enhance it for you?'

Think it's a rather descriptive term myself, sort of a posh way of saying, 'Shall I see if I can make your penis grow?'

But what if he says no? Does that mean I'm boring? Or ugly? Or fat? Or too thin? Or too hairy? Need to sort my bikini area out.

These are bizarre things to be worried about just six hours before my first shift as a high-class hooker – stuff what I'm supposed to call myself – a hooker is a hooker.

Except this is England so it really makes me a prostitute, but 'hooker' is so much easier to swallow.

Eugh.

Horrid thoughts.

*13.07*

Have a pubic rash.

The razor was blunt.

Only had Dettol to put on it. So now I have a bright red, pimply pubic rash that smells of sick and stings like hell.

Hope he doesn't want his penis enlarged.

*13.09*

But what if he does? What do I say?

Where the hell do I take him? Who pays?

Think I need to call Fiona.

*13.16*

She laughed at me.

Of course I don't have to *pay*. Silly me. If he wants 'enhancement' he will have a hotel room sorted. But I am to remember that the agency frowns upon any sexual activity and they do not condone extracurricular activity.

Weird, since they take ten per cent of anything I earn from penis enlargement.

My gentleman is from Italy. I lurve Italy! So at least I'll have something to talk about.

He is married (didn't need to know that) with three children (or that) and owns nearly all of the hotels on the Riviera. Hurrah. That bit came in handy. He's flying me . . . *flying me!!* to a country hotel somewhere in Warwickshire for dinner and whatever comes next .

Flying! In a helicopter – not that I'm averse to helicopters. I've actually flown one. Several times. I once decided that my calling in life was to be a helicopter pilot and so decided to take lessons. Eight hours of flying later and the first invoice arrived. I went off the idea after that.

But I still did it.

I know how to manipulate a cyclic lever. Only in the R22 of course, but still it's a start, and I'm sure I can work it into the conversation somehow.

After all, he may want me to manipulate his cyclic lever later.

Have drunk three-quarters of a bottle of Rioja. Still at least my pubic area doesn't sting so much. Still smells of sick though. And it's pimply.

I'll put some make-up on it if I have to.

God bless Leichner.


### 16.57

I fell asleep. I have a hangover and my pubic area is orange – the make-up didn't work. My hair however is shiny and smells lemon fresh and I managed to apply my make-up evenly despite my shaky hands. I am scared, and I no longer know who I am.


### 17.15

I have been staring at my red dress for almost twenty minutes. I can't bring myself to put it on. I am procrastinating.

I chose red on purpose. I can pretend to be Roxanne, *à la* Sting. I know Sting doesn't actually mention the colour of the dress Roxanne wears, but I always fancy that it's red.


### 17.23

Red dress on.

Goodbye Chloe.
Hello hooker.

*17.29*
He's here. I've peeked out of the window. He looks okay. At least the top of his head looks okay. Thick head of dark hair. Nice car. Don't know what it is but it's silver with the roof down. Can't see the reg number.
Pants.
I am leaving this diary plus a note detailing his description (dark hair – not receding), description of his car (silver two-seater convertible), and of course where we're going, by the front door.
Just in case I never return. I hope that's enough information. Not much to go on.
If I'm worried about never returning why am I going?
Maybe I don't care.
Or maybe I do care, but no one else does.

*17.33*
The front door is open.
I opened it.
But I can't move. I'm rooted to the spot, just staring at the hallway that lies beyond, and the stairs that will take me away from this flat and this life. The stairs that will take Chloe away from her family and friends. The stairs that just a few months ago promised a brand-new life.
I just can't bring myself to step over the threshold. Once I go, I will never return.

## 18 June

I don't know what to make of the evening. How do you measure the success of something that is pretty much preordained?

It's hardly like a first date.

The evening began. That's it really. The evening began. It wasn't like a first date when you really fancy someone and have that electric feeling all evening, the one that pretty much rests on 'will we shag or won't we'. Not that good girls do that sort of thing on first dates, of course they don't. They try to get it over and done with before the date – messes with the make-up, plus, that way, if the date is a dud he can be ditched and the search can begin for a new Mr Right. Hey presto! Two shags in one night, and a free dinner thrown in! Which of course is another lie, and I have never done it, at least not without polishing off at least three bottles of champagne, but I hear it goes on.

Nope. Escorting is not like a first date at all. Because when you hire your ass out at three thousand pounds per night including extras, there's a teeny tiny bit of added pressure.

I had no idea what to say to Toni. At least I think his name was Toni. I couldn't remember his name and hadn't written it down. Not to worry, I thought, he'll tell me.

Except, when he introduced himself, his accent was so thick that it sounded like 'Khogni'. The closest Mediterranean name I could think of that sounded like a mouthful of phlegm with 'ni' at the end was Toni. So I called him Toni. Except I didn't.

At least not to his face. Getting a client's name is a big no-no, so whenever I needed to speak to him, I lowered my head did a pretty good impression of someone clearing their throat and added 'ni' at the end of it.

Perfect. It did the trick. Hell on the vocal chords though.

161

I couldn't think of anything to say. Why is it that when I'm on my own I have a thousand and one things to say and have to have a conversation with either a TV news reporter or a piece of toast (I told it, it wasn't toasty enough), yet when I'm in the company of a man who has paid thousands to shag me, I go dumb. Actually I didn't know whether or not he wanted to shag me, but the pressure was still the same. So I didn't speak.

Fortunately, the top was down on the car and the wind gushing around my ears made conversation impossible. By the time we got to the heliport I had a stiff neck and earache.

Khogni looked rather nervous and I felt a pang of guilt. Don't know why, I just did.

As the pilot did the final checks and waited for clearance, he popped open a bottle of champagne.

'Thank God,' I thought. Champagne is enough to loosen anyone.

Halfway down the second glass and I decided it was time for me to impress my soon to be possible-maybe-Italian lover with my helicopter expertise, and maybe throw in a hint of seduction to whet his whistle.

I leant across and whispered coyly, 'I'm very good with a cyclic lever. In fact I've been told that I'm above average. I have very nimble hands, very gentle – ideal for smooth manipulation and manoeuvring.'

Unfortunately the conversation was lost on him because he didn't have his headset on and couldn't hear me above the drone of the blades.

The pilot had his on though.

Think I made his day. My gentleman, however, just smiled sweetly at me and continued to look nervous.

Deciding that silence was the better option, I sat back, hoping that the mist that had invaded my head and senses would lift.

It didn't.

The mist soon became a fog. But I'm a very good drunk, and can pretty much disguise my drunkenness and very rarely slur. It's just that sometimes I have trouble following conversations and then blah on about Roy Wood's arse almost suffocating me when I was seven. Me and my celebrity parties!

I knew I wasn't hideously drunk though, just drunk enough to feel confident to talk to my man in his native tongue.

I decided to save that treat for our meal.

Within an hour we were there.

The helicopter landed smoothly and I congratulated the pilot on his handling of the yaw peddles and cyclic lever – they really are the only bits of a helicopter I can still name, so I throw them into a conversation at any opportunity. He winked at me and blew me a kiss.

A butler ran over and took Toni's bag from him – hmm, must be planning on staying here – and another stood at the edge of the pathway with a tray holding two glasses of champagne!

Hurrah! More champagne!

The sensible thing would have been to decline.

I don't do sensible.

Never have, never will.

So I picked up a glass of champagne and sashayed into the manor-come-overly-priced-hotel/restaurant.

At least I hope it was a sashay. It could have been a stagger.

The maître d' snapped to attention as soon as he saw us and came dashing over – actually maybe his was more of a tight-assed sashay. He spoke to Toni in what I assumed was French and then Toni answered in French. I was impressed. Should have brushed up on my French as well as Italian. That would have really impressed him.

The maître d' looked at me. Well, he actually *surveyed* me, and then he smiled and said something to Toni, to which they both said 'oui oui' and raised their eyebrows and then winked at each other.

I felt like a fly being fried by a magnifying glass. But I had to cover it. I had a part to play. And boy did I now know it.

We were led to a rather secluded table that overlooked a river, and soon we were alone.

It was time for the play to begin.

I couldn't think of anything to say, so I asked him what snails smelt like. He looked slightly taken aback and then his nose crinkled, and his eyes creased and he began to giggle. That's when I realised that he was rather attractive. He had gorgeous sparkling eyes that were neither hazel nor brown, but had flecks of gold that were quite mesmerising; they were simply the most attractive eyes I had ever seen. His skin was a creamy olive colour and so smooth that I imagined, had I run my hand over his face, it would slide off – in a non-greasy sense.

But best of all he had well-manicured, large hands. I'm a bit of a hands girl. It has to do with feeling protected – which I never do, but still, one has to dream.

He looked at me, and I mean *looked* at me. He studied my face and stared into my eyes for such a long time that I had to look away, and when he was finally satisfied with whatever he saw he answered me.

'Uncooked they smell of the earth. Cooked they smell of garlic.'

'Fortunately you smell of neither.' I smiled. Too much champagne.

And so the evening progressed, if you can call what happened progressing.

After the snail conversation there was a lull. It's difficult to know what to say after having a conversation about snails.

The first course arrived and I decided that then was the time to show off my linguistic skills. I asked him in his native tongue what food he liked best.

'I like it from behind,' he answered, in English.

I was silent. Couldn't think of anything to say to that.

He then asked me, again in English, what position I liked best.

As my first gentleman, he was certainly very forward, but at least I knew I could do one of his preferred positions, so that was a plus. So, deciding to play it safe I also said, 'from behind' in a rather strangled, embarrassed voice. This was much more difficult than I imagined, but there was no point in rocking the boat. The conversation then died as he stared wistfully out across the river, a tiny smile playing at his lips.

Feeling a little uncomfortable and in great despair for my tiny little ass, I pushed on, and reverted back to Italian. I had revised Italian so I was going to use it. Goddamit.

'Do you come to England often?' I asked, feeling my way around the unfamiliar verbs.

His face lit up. At last I had pricked his attention, and he understood me.

'I have come in England many times, where do you prefer?'

Righty ho.

It was strange, being English, talking pigeon Italian to an Italian who was speaking English. I think that at some point we must have misunderstood one another, so I decided my mother tongue was safest and told him that Chester was really beautiful and he really should go when he comes again – the trouble with speaking pigeon Italian is when you revert back to English, that too becomes a little – pigeon. I've never actually been to Chester. But I have watched a few episodes of *Hollyoaks* so I felt qualified enough to say.

He told me that he agreed.

Oh goody, now we were getting somewhere.

He said that to come on the chest really was beautiful he had done it many times before and he looked forward to doing it with me later.

Tissues! I hadn't bought tissues!

By the time the main course arrived I was feeling as wilted and as sweaty as my spinach.

The hotel was airy and bright despite its Tudor appearance, but the evening sun was still hot and punishing. That coupled with my increasing embarrassment made for very sweaty armpits and a woman not fit for three thousands pounds' worth of sex. I ditched the Italian altogether, and stuck with my beloved English. I asked him why he didn't speak to me in Italian. He said he didn't really understand Italian. I asked him how come. He said there had never really been a need. What language did he speak at home then?

French.

Why?

Because that was the common language.

Hmm. Where is home?

France.

France. Not Italy then. Still, he had managed to convey a few of his favourite sexual positions to me, so at least I knew what to expect. I though about charging extra for the Italian lessons and then decided against it.

The evening progressed. I hardly touched my salmon *en croute*. Partly because it looked too pretty, but mainly because it was fishy.

Didn't think that one through.

Before the dessert arrived I excused myself and went to the bathroom to cool myself down. The marble surroundings were cool and instantly refreshing. I stood looking into the ornate mirror and barely recognised the woman staring back. The woman with the frightened eyes of a child, pleading with her to stop.

I washed the child away with a splash of cold water and then dabbed my armpits.

Bad idea.

166

The water trickled onto my red silk dress and I had to stand over a hand-dryer for ten minutes in order to dry it off.

Humidity and my hair don't mix. When humidity and my hair meet, an extra six feet of headroom is required. By the time my dress was dry I had gained several inches and my armpits were once again smelly.

Great.

When I got back to the table Toni's dessert had been and gone and my ice cream was nothing more than vanilla and pistachio soup. He gave me the once over, tried to stifle a scream – made that bit up – but I wouldn't have blamed him, and said 'I think we should come.'

I wasn't sure whether that was a grammatical error, or a request for enhancement.

For the second time that evening I thought 'shit'.

The time had come. And the little girl with the scared eyes returned and begged me not to go ahead.


## 20 June

I have had sex with a man for money.
I am a prostitute.
Why can't I feel anything?


## 25 June

Today is the sort of day that the Monkees should be playing in the background, and everyone should be walking to the happy, summery beat, and give thanks and praise for the precious elusive quality of life.
Life is great!

And I'm a prostitute.

Oh hurrah!

I ventured out today for the first time since my little 'encounter', and when God didn't strike me down with a thunderbolt, I took it as a good sign and decided to go for a stroll.

Don't generally do strolling.

Do now I'm a hooker.

See how healthy this lifestyle is?

I sauntered down the road, and I mean *sauntered*. I can actually understand now why Sophia has so much confidence; I mean, if men want to pay for my company and perhaps a little enhancement afterwards, I must be doing something right! Not that they pay Sophia, she gives it up for free. Hmm. Mustn't dwell on that!

Birds sang as I walked past them, flowers bent their heads towards me so I could appreciate their scent and children flocked around my ankles and gazed lovingly up at me. And all the time the Monkees were telling people that there I came.

At least they did in my head.

I am amazed at how easy it is to pretend that a part of my life does not exist. The whole thing has given me such a feeling of power and control that I once again feel on top of the world. 'Tis a much better situation than the scenario that runs in my head. The one where I tell everyone and anyone that I'm a prostitute.

'Morning Chloe.'

'I'm a prostitute!'

Walking past the fishmonger's. 'Morning young lady!'

'I'm a prostitute! Nice fish by the way!'

Afternoon tea with my mother and she asks, 'More cream, dear?'

'I'm a prostitute!' At which point she swoons ever so carefully onto the lawn while still clutching the best china, and then peeks through slitted eyes to see who's going to come running.

But in reality it's not like that all. I don't dwell on it too much now. That's how you deal with it. It is a job and nothing more. Given the choice between that and cleaning the hotel bedrooms that such activities take place in, I know what I'd choose.

So life was good today. In a 'didn't feel the need to occupy every second with banal activities' sort of way. Haven't been able to just 'be' for a while.

Perhaps the desperation and confusion is passing.

Hurrah!


## 7 July

It's raining.

Big fat summer raindrops that bounce off the floor and make everything grey and lifeless. The air is thick and humid and buzzes with uncharged electricity. There is a storm coming and today is going to be a black day. I should recognise the signs by now. Good days follow bad, and bad days can last forever. I have had a run of very good, very confident days and I believed that things were going to get better, that I could cope, and then a new day dawns and suddenly everything is grey again. And I can't cope.

I can only assume that everyone else believes I *am* coping; I haven't heard from anyone for a few days. On a good day that's fine, I don't care if no one calls me – I'll call them to ask how they are, to make arrangements to see them, or just to talk. I can do that on good days.

But on dirty, grey days I feel alone again, abandoned, not

worthy of friends or support. I feel disposable and I want to run away, I want to disappear.

On days like today, I need to lock myself away and hope that the clouds will part and that the sun will once again shine. I know by now that I have to wait it out, and that I will think negative thoughts about everything. I just have to be patient.

*19.00*

I feel used and worthless.

What have I been doing with my life? Why can't I take control? Only I can take charge of my life, no one else. So why am I waiting?

I'm tired. I'm tired of pretending. I want to give in, I want to lie down and go to sleep and wake up when it's all over. I've had enough.

What's so wrong in admitting that you're hurting? What's wrong with crying? What's wrong with saying you can't cope when you've lost everything?

I am walking through a storm, and I have no protection, so why not just get soaked?

Go with the flow.

No point in fighting it. It rains when you least expect it.

*21.13*

I am so angry with myself and feel so out of control that the feelings are suffocating me and there is no escape. I hate myself and I hate my world. I want to be seen, but I'm terrified of revealing the real me. Will I ever be good enough?

I want to sleep, but I can't, sleep is always punctuated by dreams or nightmares and I wake up sweating.

*22.04*

Have broken down again.

I was doing something as innocent as making a cup of

herbal tea when I curled up into a ball on the kitchen floor and cried. I can't go through this on my own any longer, but I have to. I can only rely on myself. The only person I can ever trust is me. I am alone. No one can ever understand; I was stupid enough to let this happen so I have to deal with it.

I just wish I could let people *see* me.

The *real* me. The me that *isn't* okay, the me that needs support and understanding. I want someone to talk me out of this life and put me back on track, but there is no one. There is only me, and there will only ever be me.

And what would I tell them anyway? I can never admit this life, or these actions. My life doesn't 'fit' any more, nothing goes together. I have a secret life that no one will ever know about. So I'll just put on the smile; the despair will become delight and the tears will turn to laughter and perhaps one day the rest of me will catch up and I will once again smile a real smile.

On days like this I feel such anger and frustration that I can't control myself, or my actions. The feelings are so powerful and overwhelming that they have no outlet, I want to run away from the frustration, I want to feel something other than this consuming rage and desperate hopelessness. I want to disappear, I want to change.

I want to stop doing the crazy things that I am doing. I want to escape from the girl I used to be and at the same time I mourn her; she was not worth loving; she is not worth being. I will never be her again.

This pain is immeasurable and all-consuming.

There is no escape. There is no understanding and I can only turn these feelings in on myself. I have turned a corner and find myself on a treacherous road of despair, terror and self-harm, and I have no idea where this road will lead.

I, Chloe Richards, the girl who once had it all, the girl that thought 'forever' meant just that, have lost the one thing that keeps everyone going, I have lost my hope. And in losing hope, I have also lost my self-worth. I hate myself for my lack of control and I hate these inescapable emotions, but now I have an outlet for my pain. Whenever I am suffocating beneath a blanket of loneliness and despair I take out a knife and drag it across my skin and watch as the wound appears and somehow the pain is replaced with a new, altogether different, feeling. It is horrifyingly satisfying. And I am once again in control.

When the knife is drawn across my skin and I feel the first trickle of warm blood as it escapes the wound, I feel alive. I become a different person, existing in a different world, where emotions are controlled and pain is only pain, it does not consume you, it is there simply as a release.

The pain makes me feel real again, I can exist once more, and by the time the blood has congealed and the skin has already begun to knit, the despair has eased, and I can function yet again.

As each day passes the girl in the mirror fades, and the life in her eyes slowly dies.

And I no longer care.


## 8 July

Yesterday was the blackest day I've had for a while. I should know that dizzying highs will be followed by crushing lows. I am riding a tidal wave of emotions and I have no life raft.

Today I feel silly.

Self-harm is a bad thing. Bad. Bad. Bad. Yet it releases something from deep within, it has a cathartic effect, and as the blood flows I feel a sense of perverse pleasure. I am inflicting pain to relieve pain. I am punishing myself, but in punishing *me* I wonder if there is also a part of me that is punishing *others*. I know that that makes no sense whatso-

172

ever; why would I punish others? What is that I perceive they have done? Should I really blame others simply because I can't open up to them? Or because I can't control my life? Is it their fault that I feel I am slowly disappearing and can only stand and watch helplessly as I am swept away?

Invented the word fugger.
Think it rocks, as words go. Children could say fugger and not get into any trouble, until of course society kidnaps the term and turns it into yet another swear word.
Damn society for potentially stealing my new word.


## 10 July

*10.00*
Eek! I have great ugly welts on my arms and stomach. I look like a nutter.
Maybe I *am* a nutter – what sort of person runs a knife across their skin and feels happy when they see blood?
A nutter that's who. Will never do it again. I remember reading once that Princess Di had self-harmed. Thought she was a nutter. Now I understand the uncontrollable desperation that precedes an act of self-harm.
Or is it called self abuse?

*11.03*
Think perhaps self-abuse is something altogether different, and more suited to adult entertainment. Wonder what excuses Princess Di came up with when she self-harmed? Maybe she wasn't as stupid as me. Bet she didn't pick obvious places to scar.
Like the arms.
In summer.
I'm an arse.

173

Have decided to tell people that I have befriended a neigh-bourhood cat which sometimes gets a little vicious. Think that will work. I'm so in control of everything no one will ever suspect that I drag a serrated knife across my arms and stomach.

Only nutters do that.

Am nutter.


## 15 July

*15.47*

Was having coffee outside café earlier when my phone rang, *The* phone. The hooker phone.

Didn't think it was the done thing to talk about sexual positions and payments in front of frothy-coffee-sipping middle-class pensioners, so decided the best thing to do was to ignore my phone.

But it didn't stop ringing.

Then I remembered one of the 'rules'.

'You must always answer the phone Chloe. We must always be able to contact you. If you don't, you're out.'

So I answered the phone.

And am having phone sex later.

Crikey.

Didn't even know we offered that service. Never had phone sex before. Somehow it seems dirtier than actual sex.

And scarier.

Wonder if I actually have to fiddle with my bits or if I should pretend to. How does one fiddle with one's bits when on the phone anyway?

Will pretend to fiddle.

Then again, seems like cheating if I don't actually do it.

He's paying an awful lot of money for just a few minutes'

work – Fiona says it only takes about ten minutes – so I want him to get his money's worth.

Maybe he won't actually care if I'm fiddling.

Pants.

Am novice.

Perhaps I should see how it goes, how the mood takes me.

*16.03*

Uh-oh! What if he doesn't . . . wotsit? What do I do then? Do I have to go on ooh-ing and ahh-ing all night until he does?

Perhaps I should buy Strepsils.

No.

Mustn't have mouth full. Will buy lemon and honey, and sip surreptitiously between oohs.

*16.25*

Will also buy wine. Big bottle of.

*18.33*

Have had bath and fluffed hair, and smell lemon fresh. He may not be able to see or smell me, but I can still make an effort.

What would mother think?

Goodness.

One can't have phone sex with a complete stranger without at least washing one's bits.

So am squeaky clean. Have just under two hours until he calls. Fiona said 'around eight-thirty'.

Will now open wine.

*20.45*

Wine nearly gone.

Am up for anything.

Except phone sex.
Don't think I can do it.

*20.57*
He still hasn't called. Hurrah!
Perhaps he won't.

*21.04*
Wonder if I'll still get paid? After all, I did stay in.

*21.07*
Wonder if there are any films on TV with happy, soppy
endings?
Yikes!
Phone is ringing!

*22.27*
Was him. Took longer than ten minutes. My bits remain
untouched.

*22.33*
Can't believe I've had phone sex. Don't think I did it right.
Still, I believe there was an . . . emission.
Eugh!
I heard it.
Eugh! Eugh!

*22.45*
Have had hot shower.
Eugh!

*23.00*
Okay, so I've done it. Wasn't too bad, considering. Actually
was pretty weird. Phone rang. Was going to be all sultry and
sexy voiced, so answered in what I hoped was a sexy voice.

Bit of spittle went wrong way.

Began choking. Took a minute or two before I was able to speak. By now voice was very squeaky. He asked if he should call me back. Said yes. Put phone down and didn't expect him to call back.

He did.

This time I thought it best to answer in a normal voice.

'Hello.'

'Hold it.'

'Oh, okay.' Assumed he meant 'can you please wait a moment', so I did.

Waited a long time.

He didn't say anything. Nothing at all. Didn't know what to do, or even if he was still there, so after a while I said 'Hello?'

'Are you holding it?'

'Erm, yes. Yes I'm holding it.' Crikey!!

'What does it feel like?'

Shit! Don't even know what I'm holding. Best play it safe.

'It feels big.'

'Gnngh!'

'Pardon?'

'What else? Tell me what else.'

'It feels big.' Shit! Said that! 'And erm . . . it's getting bigger.' Stick with what you know, that's my motto.

'Gnngh. What else? Tell me what else.'

'And hard?'

'Oh yes, How hard? How hard is it? What does it look like?' How the freak should I know!!

'It looks, big, and hard and . . .' have to say it, have to say it, 'shiny!'

EUGH!!

'Gnngh! What are you doing to it?'

I'm holding it of course! Pay attention man!

'Is it moving?'

Eh? Is what moving? Are we talking about the same thing here?

'Yes, it's moving.' I hope.

'How is it moving?'

'Slowly. Veery slowly, up and down.' Getting the hang of it now!

'Gnnh . . . Gnngh. Wait.'

'Oh, okay.'

So I waited.

And waited.

'Hello . . .?'

'Are you still moving slowly up and down?'

Anything you say. 'Yes.'

'What are your lips doing?' Ohh, so I'm down *there* now am I?

'My lips are sliding up and down.'

Eugh! Eugh! Eugh! It could look like a turkey neck for all I knew!

'Gnngh. Carry on. Don't stop. Tell me.' His voice was a bit croaky at this stage.

'Up and down, up and down.' Well he did say carry on.

'I have a Creme Egg.'

Eh?

'I've sucked out the centre. Do you suck out the centre of yours?'

What the freak? A Creme Egg? What was this, a how do you eat yours survey?!

'Yes, I love to suck out the centre.'

Somehow think Creme Egg sucking is euphemism for something more sinister. And less sweet.

'Tell me how you suck yours. Tell me slowly.'

Bet he's an MP!!

'Erm, I use my tongue to scoop it all up and then lick the rest.' Well I do! Never will again though!

'Ooh yes. Tell me how it tastes.'

178

'Sickly.'

'What?'

Shit! 'Sweet. It tastes really sweet and sticky and it's all around my mouth.' Eugh!

'More. Tell me more!'

'And I, erm . . .' Stuck! What more could I say? 'I, er, have to lick my lips.' Again, very true.

'My Creme Egg has no filling. I need to fill it again. Make me fill it. Talk to me until my Egg is full.'

Definitely an MP! Bet he's wearing football kit and suspenders, though most have an orange shoved in their mouth. This one has a Creme Egg on the end of his penis.

'Erm, the cream is all around my mouth. My lips are sticky, but I want more, so I lick the inside until there's nothing left. It's all in my mouth.'

EUGH!!!

Heard what sounded like person having heart attack, and then a crunching noise. He was eating his cream egg, complete with filling! He came back on the line and between mouthfuls of chocolate and erm, cream, and said, 'That was great. I'll be in touch.' Yeah, next time we'll use a fondue. Probably off to a Cabinet meeting or something.

So. Have had phone sex. And also discovered chocolate-ality.

Much better than the beastie version, but still icky.


**19 July**

My birthday!

Am busy, busy girl. Very popular. However, things are not going as planned, but then when do they? It seems that the world is full of people wanting bizarre sexual favours and they are willing to pay any amount for them.

179

Fiona has called me again, with another bizarre proposition. Why can't I just have normal requests? Like 'Does she do it doggy?' That would be nice.

This time Fiona wants to know if I 'do couples darling?'

Wasn't sure what she meant. Of course I do couples. Lots of my friends are couples. I have no problem whatsoever with couples. Couples are great. Was even one half of a couple myself for several years, not terribly successful, but still I can relate.

Was not what she meant and I suspected as much. She wanted to know if I'd ever had sex with a couple.

Couple of what?

Was procrastinating, but needed to buy myself some thinking time. So, now I was on the 'does threesomes' list was I? How on earth had I managed that?

Turns out she was desperate. This was a rather well-to-do couple who were regulars, and called her last minute, and she had no girl free, so she thought she'd give me a try.

As you do.

Pop me back on the shelf when you're done won't you?

Told her I would have to give it some extensive consideration. She has given me an hour. Apparently they want someone tonight. Obviously they suddenly felt frisky and were in need of a whore. Don't you just hate it when that happens? Prostitutes eh? Never around when you need one. So, I have an hour to think about it.

*15.01*
Not doing it.

*15.23*
Wouldn't be right. Just the thought makes me feel icky. And the logistics don't ... fit. Where do things go, and how? What are the rules?

And what if I pop my head down by the ladies' bits to have

a bit of a furtle and think, 'Eek, hope mine doesn't look like that!' Or worse, 'Crikey, mine isn't that pretty.'

And what does the man do? Where does he put his wotsit? What if his wotsit gets accidentally tangled up with my bits? Is that allowed? Or will wifey smack me in the mouth? Am I insured for damage like that?

Must check.

If I decide to go through with it that is.

### 15.37

What if I'm sick because of what we're doing?

I'm sure I would be. All those bits bobbing about. Have never been terribly good at bobbing bits. Could never go on a cruise.

### 15.53

Pants! Is it a failure if I say no? After all, I didn't sign up for this. I signed up for dinner and straight in and out missionary-style, over in ten minutes sex.

Hasn't happened yet.

Have so far had sex with a man who says I'm too innocent for this, yet wants to see me again. Have had phone sex with a Creme Egg.

And now this.

Where do I draw the line? Think the line must be drawn here. After all, what if the wife hasn't washed? I can't even walk past the fishmonger without retching. Lord knows what I'd be like with unwashed bits.

Big fat chalk line drawn here. Am not doing it.

### 16.07

Shit. Can't get hold of Fiona, am late phoning her back. Hope she hasn't taken my lateness as a positive sign. Oh my God, does that mean I have to do it now? Didn't say I would. I just didn't call her back in time. Sure I don't have to do it.

*16.10*

Still, would be a shame to stand them up, they might be looking forward to it.

*16.13*

Don't know how I'd cope if the woman had a fabulous body. Would probably hide beneath the sheets and not let them look at me.

Is that allowed?

Then again, don't want wifey to look like back end of a bus either. Hmm. Wonder if I can see a picture of them before I furtle with their bits?

*16.17*

EUGH! Have had thought.

Horrible, horrible thought!

Don't know why I didn't think of it sooner.

What if I *know* them? What would be more embarrassing? Me being a hooker, or them soliciting one for a threesome? How does one politely handle such a delicate situation? Bet Sophia would know.

*16.27*

Do not have to face horrible situation. Have got hold of Fiona. Told her I'm not doing it. She said, 'Not to worry darling, I'll do it myself, about time I got back into the swing of things.'

Blimey! The things that go on behind closed doors.

**5 August**

Am still a busy girl.

Saw 'Toni' again. Think he's got a bit of a soft spot for me. I don't mind, at least he's almost normal.

182

Some of the requests I get are most bizarre, and usually refused.

Anyway, Catherine and I are off to see a spiritualist or medium or something. This person is very well known on the cable TV networks. Amazingly accurate, so I'm told.

Have never really understood spiritualists, or the people that go to see them.

I understand them now.

I want to know where I'm going, where I'll end up. I want to know everything will be okay. So, I'm going, and I don't care what people say.


## 27 August

People have been laughing at me because I'm going to see a spiritualist.

I don't care.

One friend of mine who has recently refound God and become a Christian has told me not to go. Said the 'people' talking to the spiritualists were really demons pretending to be people we know.

Asked him how he knew this.

He said his faith told him.

Asked him who he had faith in.

Said Jesus.

Asked if Jesus was a spirit.

He said yes.

So I asked how he knew that Jesus was really the spirit talking and not some nasty demon doing an impression.

He said he just knew, said you can tell when 'the Lord is talking'.

Asked him if the Lord had ever spoken to him.

No.

Who does the Lord talk to then?

Went very quiet, so I persisted and asked how, if the Lord only spoke to a select few people, he could categorically say it was Jesus, and not those nasty demon spirits he claims exist.

No longer have friend who is a Christian. Have a very confused friend who is now going on 'retreat' to find his faith.

Or himself.

Or something like that.

Was only trying to prove a point. I have no time for people who just accept things. You should always ask questions. You should control the flock, not follow it. Am the same with the silly people who say that cats can only see in black and white. How do they know! I know about the optical differences between a cat's eyes and humans – but it's a freaking cat – of course it's going to be different. Until a cat slinks up to me, hops on my lap and says, 'You know what, Chloe? Those scientist guys were right. We cats really can only see in black and white' I will maintain my thoroughly researched and well-debated argument.

'Have you ever been a cat?'

If the answer is no, then sod off.

Think I can be very annoying at times, I really wind people up. Gets a reaction though.

Hurrah!

So am off to see a demon charmer tomorrow. Hope he talks to me. Then again, if he does talk to me, does that mean I'll come home with a poltergeist?

Would be someone to talk to, I suppose. Hear they're mischievous little buggers, think we would get on fine. Would be a very cheap burglar alarm if nothing else.

So, good news all round.

*16.46*

Shit! What if this demon charmer lets my little secret out?

184

Eek!

The event is being televised! I could be 'out-ed' by a dead person on national TV.

Bugger.

Can see it now, 'Hmm, is there a whore in the house? No? Well, I'm definitely getting images of a young woman rutting for money – good Lord, you do have a plethora of positions my dear. Do they teach you that at slut school?'

*18.00*

I think perhaps I'm beginning to be a little too frivolous in far too many areas of my life. I'm not taking anything seriously. It seems I have moved from one extreme to the other. Just a few months ago I had a good job, a marriage, property, a future, and security. Now I'm having sex for money and living in rented accommodation, and have no idea where I'm going. And seem to care even less. And all because my husband's penis went on its holidays.

I wonder if I actually do care, but I just think 'what's the point?' If there is one thing I've learnt it's that you cannot control anything in life. If it's meant to be it will be.

Though Lord only knows why I'm on the prostitute road.

Prostitute.

Me.

I am a prostitute.

*20.05*

Hope mother never finds out. How would she? It's not like I'm going to write a book about it.

That would be stupid.

*23.00*

Must banish all thoughts of prostitution before tomorrow night. I can't have the demon charmer picking up on it. Will think Laura Ashley and fruit-picking thoughts.

185

There I go being frivolous again. No wonder people don't see me when they look at me, I don't even know who I am any more.


## 29 August

*08.33*
Well good Lord! Praise be and halleluiah! Everything is going to be fine.
Have been told so by a dead person.
The spiritualist picked me!
He says I have a 'difficult' time ahead of me, but if I can get through that I am promised much happiness.
Deep joy!
I was just sitting in the large auditorium surrounded by lots of people minding my own business when he started talking to me. It all began very innocently.
The spiritualist – whose name, rather boringly, is Dave – was on stage all alone. Except of course for his invisible sidekick Al – Al is his personal spirit guide who talks to other spirits and then to Dave, or something like that. I don't know where Al was. I imagine he floats around making invisible friends and then when he finds one with some juicy info he reports back to Dave. Could be wrong though.
Anyway, the lights dimmed and the performance began. Dave stood perfectly still on the dark stage bathed in a bright light. Looked very celestial, but was in fact aided by the props and lighting department. He stood with his head lowered and the audience was perfectly quiet waiting to see what would happen. Suddenly his head lolled from one side to the other, and he began talking. 'Yes okay, okay.' He then lifted his head and looked directly at me. 'Yes, yes I see her. Al, you're sure? You're absolutely sure?'
EEEK!

186

Al had obviously answered in the affirmative because Dave walked over to the edge of the stage and stood gazing at me. At least I assumed it was me, could have been the woman behind, but his eyes were generally pointed in my direction. I was totally unprepared and began to panic. What was he going to say? What if I didn't know any of the people he spoke about?

Catherine gave me a dig in the ribs and hid half of her face. 'Oh my God, what's he going to say? I can't look!' she hissed into my shoulder.

Was very afraid and wanted to go home.

Dave then pointed at us and said, 'I have a George coming through, it's very recent.'

Didn't know what he meant. What was recent – his talk with George? Did he and George talk often? So often in fact that Dave had to qualify the fact that this conversation was recent? Thought it odd that George would have conversation with strange man for no reason, thought talking drained one's energy when one was dead. But could be wrong though – am not dead, have however watched *Ghost*.

Got thoroughly caught up in the moment and said 'Yes, yes! It's me!'

Cath gave me sidelong look.

Dave then asked if George's passing had something to do with his chest.

'Yes!' How on earth did he do it – how did he know? It was amazing.

Dave told me that George was fine.

Ah bless. Little George was fine.

Dave then went on to say that George had been met by William and they were having a great time catching up with each other.

Was very, very pleased.

Nice to know that Dave and William have found one another again and are reminiscing about when they weren't dead.

Dave then moved on to another section and gave words of comfort and hope to several more people, and then it was the interval.

Neither Catherine nor I wanted a drink so we stayed in our seats. So did the old lady behind us and her friend. Old lady was little deaf so we were privy to her conversation. She was saying to her friend that it was such a shame that her husband *George* – who had died so recently – hadn't come through to talk to her, and wasn't it a coincidence that *her* George had a brother called William, just like that nice young lady in front. I hunkered down in my chair and hoped that Catherine hadn't heard the conversation, but she had.

She hissed at me and asked if I knew anyone called George or William.

Said no.

She asked why I had lied.

Said I thought my mum might know them and that I planned to ask her later and that if I said no I might have stopped the flow of information and missed out on some other vital info.

Am bad, bad person. Have stolen a dead husband.

Catherine dissolved into a fit of giggles and couldn't control herself. I just felt like a shit. As in a bad person; not in actually wanting to do a thingy.

Dave came back on stage after about half an hour, and did the same thing again. Middle of stage, lights out, bathed in celestial glow, head shaking, and once again over to me.

Uh-oh!

This time was not going to steal someone's dead relative. He came right over to the edge of the stage and made a joke. 'I'm back to you my love, what did your relatives do, hire a ghost ship to bring them in?'

Gave polite nervous laugh to make him feel better about the

188

bad joke. No one else laughed. Looked like a prat with no sense of humour.

Still he ploughed on undeterred. 'I have a lady standing right behind you, she is making the sign of the cross. That's a good thing.'

Hurrah!

He looked at me expectantly and I looked around to see if anyone was nodding in excitement. No one was – they were all looking at me.

Uh-oh.

Dave then started having a conversation with Al. 'Yes, yes all right Al. All right. I'll ask her.' Back to me. 'Remember the donkey derby?'

Crikey, yes I did.

When I was about eleven I went to donkey derby with my gran and aunt and cousin Jenna, who is four years younger than me. Donkey derby started off great. Three trots in however and Jenna came flying off – not too impressive for a girl who had horse-riding lessons, eh Jenna? I however was managing wonderfully, except the saddle had a bit of a problem: it came loose and started slipping. So I did the sensible thing and slipped with it. It slipped very slowly to the left and the only thing I could do was grab hold of the reins and cling on for dear life. Which made my donkey walk in circles and get in the way of the other donkeys and knock more children off. Pretty soon there was pandemonium. Jenna was screaming, parents were either laughing at the hilarity of it all or screaming as their child came flying off a donkey, and the donkeys themselves, well, I think they were retired after that. So yes, I remembered the donkey derby. But so could anyone. Everyone's been to a donkey derby at some point in their life.

So I remained silent.

Dave sighed and again chatted to Al. Then he tried again. 'This lady is telling me that she knows.' Right-o, that's nice.

189

Knows what? Didn't say that, just thought it in my head, but Dave answered!

'She knows that you fell off your donkey and were injured, but they didn't notice, and you kept it from them.'

SHIIIT!!!!! How did he know that? If this lady was who I beginning to think she was, how did she know?

'They told her when she crossed, and now she's telling you in order to validate who she is. She wants to pass a message on. It's very important.'

Fuck. Who was in my head? Who was listening to me? Shit. Damn – shouldn't swear. Dead people listening.

'It appears you need more validation. Okay.' He cocked his head to one side and then began laughing. 'I can say this to her?' he asked Al. 'Really, it's a bit embarrassing. Okay then.' He turned back to me and tried to stop laughing. 'I'm being shown an image of you aged about thirteen, you're on stage and you're singing, except . . . you're . . . erm, you appear to . . .'

Okay, didn't need him to say any more or give anything else away, time to admit.

'It's my grandmother. I think.'

'She says it is.'

Began to cry. Loved my gran. Missed her almost daily for the past fifteen years, was there when she died, we were all there. We all loved her. And miss her. Didn't like it any more, it wasn't fun any more, I wanted to go home. And I wanted to stop crying!

But good old Dave knew when he was onto a good thing and he carried on.

'She says you have to be strong. You have to put all those negative thoughts away. You will get through this. You are going through a dark time, a very dark time. And it will get worse.'

Hurrah! More shit for the fan! Didn't think they were

190

allowed to say bad things!! Great, no point me getting out of bed in the near future!

Dave then looked at me full of concern, before once again checking in with Al – which gave me enough time to stop crying and I realised that I was squeezing Catherine's hand.

Dave was chatting to Al for a while and there was a murmur that rang throughout the audience and they all looked at me. Like the frightened animal I was.

Finally Dave came back to me. 'You have been having very black thoughts. They say that you have almost given up. You mustn't. There are great things waiting for you. You have to continue on the road you're on.' *Don't mention the fruit-picking*!!!

Anyway, what freaking road? I wasn't on a road, I was on a bridle path covered with thorns and horse shit.

'You have to continue this way, it *will* clear. You've got a long way to go, and it's not going to be easy, but you'll get there.' He was about to walk away when he stopped, his back was to us and he spoke to Al again. When he turned around his face was rather pale, and I began to freak out inside. My stomach performed outlandish somersaults and, surprise, surprise, I needed the loo.

He looked directly at me and said, 'You have to pay attention to what I am going to say, okay?'

Catherine gripped my hand and I nodded.

'You have to remember that no matter what happens to you, she will be there. You have to remember that she is there. You have to be strong. You have a hard time ahead my darling, you are going to make some decisions that you will regret, but they will lead you to your future, if you let them. You have the chance of a wonderful future. But you're in charge of your own destiny. Not everyone agrees with that, but I'm here to tell you that you are. She'll be there, and you not only have her blessing, but you now have mine. I know what you've done, and what will happen as a result of

191

this chosen path, but you will get through it. And they want me to let you know that they hear you. Every night, without fail. They hear you.'

Cue enormous amounts of tears and a lot of toilet visits.

What the hell was going to happen to me? What was it going to be: a rosy future or roses at my funeral?

Did not stay to hear the end, had to leave. Am never ever going to one of those demon charmers ever again. But I must try to look on the bright side: I have a chance of a good future. Will *not* make any bad decisions, I will be sensible and grown up.

Hurrah!

Am in charge of my destiny! Will have rosy future. Not roses at my funeral. And must not ever again steal a dead husband.

Dead husband stealing is bad.


## 1 September

Had date last night. No enhancement required. Have also had phone sex with the Creme Egg guy. This time he had a finger of fudge, though I suspect it wasn't particularly fudge-y at the end.

Seems the shock is wearing off now.

Perhaps I'm becoming indifferent to it all.


## 27 September

Nothing rosy happening yet.

Will be very patient.

Most things happen when you least expect them to and you never know what's around the corner and he who laughs last laughs longest, and other such nonsense.

Am not the most patient person on earth.
Am going to go out and drink wine and wait for something rosy to finally happen. Perhaps I will drink *rosé* wine. Or pink wine as it should be called – 'tis pink after all.


## 29 September

Find myself running to the front door each morning and looking for post. Don't know what I'm expecting to find as not many people know where I live, and I haven't written to anyone, but somehow think that the post is my salvation. I fancy that someday, someone will write to me and tell me how much they love me and that they can't live without me and have been waiting their whole life for me, they just didn't realise it.

See myself as a bit of a Nicole. A Nicole awaiting her Ewan perhaps. Don't know what I would do if someone did tell me they loved me. Cry probably. And then put up the defence barrier.

It's okay for *me* to love someone, but not okay for them to love me back. If they love me it means they'll expect things of me, and I'll just let them down and then I'll be all crying and lonely again.

So I'm not going to let anyone love me.

Best that way.


## 5 October

Have another gentleman booked for tomorrow.

He has only just been accepted by Fiona and has not yet used her services – or mine as the case may be – and I have to report back to her once I'm done.

Or he's done.

Whichever is first.

Which will be him.

I'm never done.

Eugh! Not while on the job.

His name is Frankie, which rather concerned me because only men in their eighties are called Frankie, and I don't do wrinklies. Plus I don't know a thing about heart resuscitation. Said as much to Fiona.

'Oh darling, he's thirty-five if he's a day.' Really don't understand that saying.

Then she told me where he was taking me!

Hurrah!

Am going to swanky wedding complete with Hollywood actress and other celebs.

Hurrah!

Am going as hooker-type person.

Hurrah!

Hope *Hello!* aren't there. How would I explain that to mother?

'Darling, what are you doing on the back pages of *Hello!* And where are your clothes? Did you know there would be photographers? Oh darling, what did I tell you about matching underwear? If you're going to be caught semi-naked draped over a sex-hungry man then you must always choose the right underwear. Now about the young man you were with, was that really . . .'

Doesn't bear thinking about, it would be dinner party heaven for her.

The 'gentleman' concerned has asked Fiona for a young lady who wouldn't come across all star-struck.

And she chose me.

Obviously remembered the Roy Wood sitting on face incident – handled that very professionally even though I was only seven. Knew it would get me somewhere one day.

Was a little puzzled by Fiona's questioning. Appears that she

194

hasn't used this 'gentleman' before; he has come by 'word of mouth' and she was rather worried. 'Darling, you will call me the moment you get home won't you?' Why on earth would I do that? I haven't had to in the past. Still I said yes. Anything to keep the boss happy. 'And remember that if anything happens and you want to leave, then you must let me know. You don't have to stay if you feel uncomfortable. Okay?'

Was getting a tad worried by this point, but again agreed.

She then told me who the 'gentleman' was.

Eek!

So swanky wedding here I come.

Must go and buy posh frock. Green I think. Possibly a hat as well.

*15.03*
And shoes!

*15.04*
And a bag!

*15.07*
Might go and get proper fake tan, not a home job that streaks and stains.

*18.00*
Read lots of Jackie Collins books when I was about three. Wonder if celeb parties are really like that?

Crikey. What do I do if more than one person wants a go?

*18.33*
Can't believe that I just wrote that. What sort of mentality do I have? Of course no more than one person can have 'a go'. Am not a prostitute.

*18.37*
Yes I am. But am not a whore, and will not allow anyone to treat me as such.

*18.39*
Yes I am.

*18.40*
Shit.
Getting depressed again.

*23.05*
Bugger, shit, fuck and fugger!! Stupid! Stupid! Stupid! Why do I do it! Goddamn it!


**6 October**

Have dirty great welt across my stomach. How the hell am I going to explain that?
'Am human pincushion, please feel free, I'm into S&M.'
Won't work.
Pants! Pants! Pants!!

*11.03*
Have fake tan booked, perhaps that will cover the scar. Then I'll go and buy a dress that will cover my stomach. Must not offer any 'enhancement' this evening, it is at my discretion anyway.
That's what I'll do.
Easy.

*15.00*
Fake tan was horrible experience. You have to stand naked in a booth on a silver disk and pretend you're about to rev

a motorbike. Must have looked very attractive – naked, crazy-haired biker chick complete with great ugly scar. Perhaps I could audition for ZZ Top video.

Once you have adopted the said position, you have to shuffle forwards and press the 'start' button. That's when the trouble begins. Because I had to shuffle forward like an extra from *Day of the Dead* in my biker pose, it meant I had to shuffle back in the same position. I couldn't find the silver disk so I had to look down. It was at this point that the machine started spraying me with its fake tan and got me square in the head, missing my face and upper body. I panicked and stood where I was, hoping that at least I was near the little silver disc, and waited for the machine to spray me again. Didn't realise that the cap covering my hair had slipped. By this point I was hyperventilating a little; 'tis very difficult to breathe in small confined booth that is spraying you with chemicals, so I stopped breathing.

Nearly fainted so had to breathe again just as the spray was hitting my face. Had mouthful of chemicals and began to choke.

Horrible, horrible experience! Am not a fan of fake tan. Did get delightful little dress though. And shoes and handbag and hat.

Shopping no longer fills the void though.

Am still empty.


*16.07*
Fuck. Have perfect white line on my forehead where the cap fell. Will have to colour it in with make-up.


*16.14*
Double fuck. Scar on my stomach is no longer red.
It is deep orange, and almost glows in the dark.
Definitely no enhancement later.

*16.17*
Have decided to take my diary with me and sneak off at opportune moments to make notes. I mean diary entries. Not notes. Notes makes it sound as if I'm going to sell a story to the tabloids.
Hmm . . .

*16.19*
No!!

*18.32*
Am all dressed up now and ready for my performance.
Dress looks good. Not too tarty. Not too conservative. Just enough to get me onto the back pages of *Hello!*
Underwear very expensive and matching – mum will be proud.

*18.37*
I'm off!

*21.00*
Crikey the champagne here is jolly good!
Feeling rather squiffy.
Terribly posh do while at the same time being rather normal. These people do normal things like drink beer and tell rude jokes and discuss the size of breasts – except they all have enhanced breasts and the men appear to be divided: those that don't give a stuff whether they're real or not as long as they are BIG, and those that think it's rather sad.
I'm liking all the men in the sad camp. Have spoken to oodles of celebs and they actually spoke back!
Am celeb friend extraordinaire.
Have lost 'gentleman' friend. He gives me the creeps anyway so I don't really care; rather possessive and very hands on, have a bruise around my wrist where he gripped me in order

to stop me walking away from him. Not that I was going to, I know how to do my job, but his grip tightened and he pulled me to him and whispered in my ear, don't know what he said, sounded like, 'If you don't do as I ask I'll tell everyone you're a bore.'

Am not a bore. Am very witty person lost in a bizarre world of sex and celebs.

Have been wondering what he meant. Think perhaps I misheard him and I should substitute the word 'bore' for another less complimentary word.

Never mind.

Will drink more champagne and be a good girl.

Perhaps I should go and look for him before he tells people how 'boring' I am.

## 21.55

Found him!

He was in the bathroom doing something with someone; didn't like to ask. Came out all moody, looked at me as though I was the devil and then grabbed me by the hand and told me to remember who was paying for whom and that I was to keep my mouth shut. Don't know what I'm supposed to keep my mouth shut about.

Don't like him. Not offering him any enhancement at all.

Fucker.

Am I to keep my mouth shut all night I wonder? Will appear very rude if I don't talk to people. Perhaps he didn't mean it like that.

Am pissed.

Can't not talk when I'm pissed.

## 22.37

Hurrah! Have had conversation and a bit of a boogie with very famous British Hollywood actress. She is very nice and terribly pretty, her skin is like alabaster and she literally glows. Asked her what make-up she used in order to glow like an angel and she laughed at me and said that she liked my dress.

Me!

My dress!

From very famous Hollywood angel!

Was not sure how to take it at first, so just looked at her waiting for something nasty or sarcastic to be said. At least I hoped I was looking at her, there were several 'hers' to choose from. Darn good champers. She then told me who had designed my dress and that she had several of her 'wonderful creations'.

Am Hollywood friend.

Oh hurrah!

And me dancing with her really pleased my 'gentleman'.

He shuffled over to us both and introduced himself to her and they had a rather short conversation, but one that seemingly pleased him. He told me that he had been trying to talk to her all evening, and all he had to do was get a 'whore to do his bidding'.

Don't like him.

Nasty man.

He then put his arm around my waist and held me tightly and walked me off the dance floor and told me I was to stay in the house and wait for him, and under no circumstances was I to move. He said we were leaving but he had to 'sort' something first. To anyone watching he must have looked very loving and attentive, but his eyes were glazed and manic, and I felt a stab of fear. How can I say no to someone like this?

What if he doesn't listen?

Will knee him in the nuts.

Am afraid, and a little angry, and very drunk.

Will call Fiona. I want to leave.

*23.00*
Can't get hold of Fiona, phone won't work and I'm too squiffy to figure out why. Am hiding in toilet; need to make escape plan. Will have little sleep first.

*23.29*
Shit! Marble floors are not very comfortable to sleep on. Head throbs and mouth feels like sandpaper. Cannot get hold of Fiona, or anyone else for that matter. At least I know why now – no signal that's why! Knew a sleep would help.
Pants!
Eek. Loud banging on door.
Fuck. Fuck. Fuck. It's him! He's angry. Double fuck – I moved!
I didn't stay where he told me to. I moved and then I fell asleep!
Shit.
Will hide here till hell freezes.
Am scared. Have started to cry and for some reason I want my mum. Don't want to go out there, my mum would know what to do, she'd deal with him. Nasty little man.
Shit.
So scared.
Still no signal.
What do I do? Do I tell him now, in front of everyone, that I'm going home alone and then insist on a taxi? Fiona won't be happy. Might give her business a bad reputation if I say something in public, so can't do that. Perhaps I should just offer him his money back – Fiona would understand. I'd give her my ten per cent so she wouldn't lose out.
Shit what do I do?

*23.34*
He's getting angrier. I can hear the rage in his voice, he almost sounds manic. Will have to go out and face him.

Once I've stopped crying and shaking.

Will think of something. Always do. Will open the door and deal with the situation. There is nothing I cannot handle. What's the worst that can happen?

## 7 October

I have bruises covering my body. There are bite marks on my shoulder and scratches covering my back. I feel dirty and useless.

I had no idea what to do, there isn't a training manual for this job, and if there was I doubt it would cover a situation like that. Maybe I should have read the signs better; they were there, any idiot would have seen them, but I only deal with words, and he made no mention of his predilection toward rough sex.

I didn't say no. I should have said no. But then maybe he would have taken that as part of the game. So I just let him, until it was over.

Shit.

How can I tell anyone about what happened? What do I do now? Where do I go? Who do I turn to? Will anyone ever understand the reasons behind my actions?

Would anyone care?

*20.00*

I remember at one point feeling so much pain that I told him to stop, but he didn't hear me. And then the garden faded and all sound disappeared until there was only pain, and I knew that there was no point in asking him to stop. He was no longer listening, so I switched off and I waited for it to be over, and for the pain to stop.

Except the pain hasn't stopped. The pain will never stop. Not now. I have turned myself into a victim. I have allowed

202

one bad experience to change my whole life and each turn I make, each step I take, leads me further away from life, and living. I am no longer in control of anything, I am not living, I am existing, and somewhere along the way I stopped caring about myself, and what happens to me. I am not beyond loving; I have just chosen to believe that I am beyond being *loved*. If last night has proved one thing, it is that I *do* care. I deserve to be loved, to be wanted to be held to be protected, and one day someone will deserve to have me love them.

There is no shame in love.

I just have to heal first.


## 8 October

I called Sophia.

She called Fiona.

Fiona called me.

She has removed the client from her list. He has offered me more money. Fiona took it on my behalf.

It appears that he is worried about my discretion. As if I want anyone to know what I've done, what I allowed him to do to me. The money is tainted; I've already been paid for my sins, I don't need anything extra. But Fiona has said she will post it to me nonetheless. Whatever she wants, I don't care, I don't particularly want the money.

I don't want these bruises either. I don't want this never-ending pain. I don't want anything.

I just want to be left alone.

Fiona said I should take a month off, in order for the bruises to heal. She has booked me an appointment with her doctor. Apparently he's very discreet.

I don't care. I'm not going.

I'm not going anywhere.

Except into another hot bath. Perhaps I can scorch away the pain and watch the memories evaporate in the steam.

The flat is perfectly still. No music, no TV, just the sound of living. And with living comes tears, and despair and abandonment.

## 9 October

People have been calling me, leaving messages, and knocking at my door, but I don't want to speak to anyone yet. I ignore all the calls and the knocking at my door.

I'm not here. I don't exist. I don't want to exist. Not as the person I have allowed myself to become. I'm so annoyed with myself. I can't stop crying, how did I let it come to this? For God's sake why can't I take control of my life?

I'm no longer living, I'm just existing.

I *will* get better. I *will* come through this. I *will* be happy again. I *will* find that elusive emotion that is buried deep within each of us. I *will* find my hope again. I will *not* be beaten. I will ride this out, however long it takes. I will grab hold of the reins and I will hang on for dear life, no matter how many hurdles I fly over, no matter how many times I become airborne, I will *never* let go of the reins. They are bound around my wrists and have become my lifeline.

## 13 October

*09.30*

Haven't written in here for days. I haven't really got anything to say and doubt that words could ever fully express what I feel inside. I don't feel real, not any more. I feel as though I've been away, far, far away, but now I'm back and I have to live with the consequences of my actions, take responsibility for what happened.

It was just rough sex.

I didn't say no – not really.

*10.57*

It was all just a game, and believing that makes it a little easier to live with. It was just rough sex. He really had no idea that that he was being *too* rough, that I was genuinely afraid. To him it was just a game. *I* was just a game. Everything beforehand had been foreplay to him, the man-handling, the crassness, the hair-pulling; it was all just part of the bigger game.

So that's how I'll deal with it. I was just a disposable part in a sick man's game. And *I* put myself there and *I* accepted the money. So it's time to move on and learn from my mistake.

*12.15*

I'll move on in a few days. Too tired to move on. Have been sleeping oodles lately. Have no idea why, I'm just sooo tired. Will sleep.

*15.17*

Have slept; still feel tired. I wonder if I sleep to erase the memories, and therefore make living easier? I have been existing for the past few days, not living as such, merely 'being'. On the surface I am the same Chloe, but inside I'm someone else. I don't know who yet, but we have been introduced. The person on the inside is harder than I am, and she doesn't care about anyone or anything. She's frivo-lous and carefree and she lives the stereotype that life has thrown at her. She is what people want her to be. What people expect her to be.

I think I have always known her, she has been nurtured and

groomed and solicited for months, and she is the person I can hide behind when things get too much and I feel life is becoming too hard and too real. She is my protection and also my downfall.

*18.35*
Have opened a bottle of Pinot Grigio. It was bought on my honeymoon, and for some reason I've been reluctant to open it.
Sod it. It's open now!

*19.58*
Rather nice bottle of wine, shame it's nearly gone. Talking of things that have gone; where did my childhood go? What happened to innocence? Does it really exist? Where is the hope that once got me through? Is hope the only thing that gets anyone through?
Hope sucks. I don't have any any more. Not even a teeny bit. It has been slowly but surely stolen, or given away with an open and trusting heart, until now there is nothing left of it.
At least that's my 'feeling sorry for me' opinion. I know that there is no rainbow, no pot of gold. No hope.

*21.00*
Have opened another bottle of wine. Could only find red wine. Am mixing my grapes. Hurrah!

*21.40*
Grapes are well and truly mixed!
Am a bit sloshed.
Perhaps that's why I no longer know the woman that stares back at me as I look in the mirror, but I cry for her every day, and for all that she has lost. There is sadness in her eyes, and I know that she is looking for answers.

She wants to know, 'Where are we going to?'
On the surface she has everything, but inside she is dying,
month by month, day by day, second by second.
And so I am dying with her.
And I no longer care.


## 19 October

The bruises have faded.
The pain has gone.
The emotional scars are beginning to heal.
I will recover.
It's time to move on.

And that's it. That's all I wrote about my engagement, my marriage break-up, my prostitution. It really was time to move on.

It was The End.

Except it wasn't.

Not quite . . .

It takes a catastrophic event to throw our lives into disarray and another to make us stand back and look at ourselves. And it's all part of life. And we all have a part to play in how we get to where we are. At some point we have to stop feeling sorry for ourselves and start dealing with what has been thrown at us.

After weeks of mourning – and that's what it was – I finally realised that I really did want to heal. The months of hurt, disappointment and pain had bubbled beneath the surface for too long and they finally exploded. I existed in a fog of confusion and pain, but this time it was different: this time I wanted to feel the pain, I *wanted* to cry, because I wanted to heal, but I couldn't. Every time I felt low, every time I felt the tears sting my eyes, something stopped me from giving in to them. I became numb.

Days merged into weeks and soon the weeks became months until it was December once again. My diary remained blank; its empty pages reflected nothing but the blessed emptiness that I felt.

I didn't make a single entry.

I refused to hide from my emotions, I didn't run away. The frivolous entries stopped. I didn't know how to be frivolous and upbeat, except of course with a 'gentleman', and there were still plenty of those.

That was the one thing I couldn't stop: I needed to feel the validation that comes with being paid lots of money for sex.

I still self-harmed, but only occasionally, and I learnt how to disguise the marks. I knew where on my body to drag the knife so the scars wouldn't be seen, but one day the release it bought wasn't quite the same, and I felt ashamed of myself for succumbing to the temptation, and slowly I stopped, and it was then that I realised I did in fact want the fairytale ending. I was placing myself in a situation that I wanted to be rescued from, and I wouldn't stop until someone told me I was worthy enough to stop.

I wanted to be rescued. I wanted the white knight, but most of all I wanted to give in. I wanted to close my eyes and wake up when it was all over.

But of course, fairytales endings don't exist. Unless your name's Cinderella or Snow White or Victoria Beckham.

I carried on as normal. I shopped for presents surrounded by happy couples and stressed families, and I felt nothing. No remorse for my actions, no tinge of regret or nostalgia for my previous Christmases, no sadness, and no optimism.

It was as though I had been thrown off the merry-go-round that is life, and I could only watch as the world span past in front of me and wouldn't let me on. Occasionally it would slow down and I could stow myself away, but eventually I would be thrown back off again.

So I found myself waiting; I *would* get on the merry-go-round, and this time I would stay on it.

And it was while I was waiting for it to slow down that my world began to slowly change, and one day, completely out

of the blue, and in the most unlikely of guises, I was
rescued . . .


## 8 January

*08.34*
I have woken up with a spring in my step, and a skip in my
heart. I feel optimistic. For the first time in ages I feel as
though I *do* have a future, I *will* be happy.
Can't imagine why I feel this way, but I'd forgotten how
wonderful it can feel just to feel so 'light'.
Perhaps I'm one step closer to taking control again.

*12.37*
Fiona has called. I have a date tonight. For some reason I
don't have that awful indescribable feeling in the pit of my
stomach.
I should have.
My date is with a child.
Good Lord.

*12.50*
Actually he's not child at all, he's twenty-four. So that would
make him a teenager then.
Crikey.
Am Mrs Robinson.

*13.00*
Hope I'm not his first.
Hmm.
Didn't consider this scenario – me as the teacher. Not sure
I'm comfortable with that.
Always assumed that I would be enhancing men of a certain
age, who were dab hands at the sport of sex but who

couldn't get it at home any longer. Never ever, ever did I think I would be doing it with a young boy.

Or young man.

Is impossible to say 'young man' and not have Kathy Burke's voice ringing in my head.

Am a dirty old woman.

*14.03*

Am also most confused. Why isn't he out getting pissed and shagging anything with a pulse?

Bet he's a freak. Bet he doesn't have any friends to go out and get pissed with. Bet he harbours anti-women thoughts. Bet he's got a great big fuck off kitchen knife under his bed. Bet he brings it with him.

Eek.

Have date with Jason.

Will end up at Lake Crystal dangling from tree with a pair of hedge cutters stuck in my throat.

Will call Fiona.

*15.03*

Am silly. Do not have a date for enhancement at all.

Just have a date.

He doesn't want any enhancement.

Hurrah!

He just wants to practise his chat-up technique.

I am to pretend that I haven't met him before – easy peasy – haven't met him. And I am to pretend that he hasn't paid me to be his date – easy peasy – I'd rather forget that anyway. And I am to give him feedback on his chat-up lines. Eek. Don't like the idea of that. Am not agony aunt. Do not know how to be negative.

Will tell him his chat-up lines are wonderful even if he tells

211

me he collects fuck off big kitchen knives and loves to jab women in the throat with hedge trimmers and leave them dangling from trees at Lake Crystal.

Will say, 'That's so interesting, do tell me more.'

Am crap at nasty. Unless of course provoked.

Fugger.

Am nervous. Would much rather shag and go.

*15.24*

Shit. What if he decides he *does* want enhancement after all and then I have to give him feedback on that as well? What if a poodle has a bigger penis than him? Will tell him he's hung like a donkey.

What if he doesn't actually manage to do anything, because he's a bit . . . keen? Will tell him all women like to have men's stuff all over them.

What if it's over in seconds? Will tell him that that all women would rather it be over seconds – gives them more time to concentrate on shopping lists.

Am creating a monster.

*16.00*

He has called.

Sounds very mature for his age, with a rather nice, soothing voice. I am to meet him inside the local museum. How very cultured and refined.

The museum is open until ten o'clock once a week in an attempt to lure more customers.

Seems to be working.

Have never had a date in the museum before, which is a shame.

Love it in the museum. They have a mummy in there at the moment, a real live mummy. Except it isn't live of course. On account of it being dead and mummified. But it's great. They also have a mummified cat, and a bird and an owl – so

212

that would be two birds – and other dead things. The cat looks a bit weird. Not a cat shape at all: it's elongated and very thin and its little tail is scrawny and pathetic. Poor little pussy cat, hope it wasn't killed on purpose just to have its brains sucked out and be wrapped in bandages to keep the dead person company.

Silly Egyptians, killing pussy cats like that. Thought the Egyptians were meant to worship cats, being as the cats kept the food free from rats and things? Perhaps the cat died first and they got some bloke off the street and killed him and sucked his brains out of his nose and wrapped him in bandages in order to keep the dead cat company.

Ah. That's nice. Much better. Love the Egyptians.

Fiona says that Fred – that's his name – is a multi-millionaire. Self-made. Something to do with computers and the internet. Which means he never goes out, and never sees daylight. Which also means he'll be podgy and pale with stunted growth and look like one of the *Flowers in the Attic* children.

Great! Have date with a mini-Jason. Asked Fiona how Fred would know it was me. Did I have to wear a rose or carry a paper or something?

Silly me.

He's seen a picture of me hasn't he, that's how he chose me.


*19.15*
Right. Am off to have a date with a virgin and tell him how great his shit chat-up lines are.


*23.45*
Am back.

Was nice.

Did not look like Jason at all. Or any of the *Flowers in the Attic* children. In fact he was rather nice looking and when he approached me I didn't even know it was him, not that I

213

knew what he looked like, he just looked a bit older than twenty-four – a bit more 'lived in' – so I didn't think it was him.

Was standing looking at a painting called *Night with her Train of Stars* by Edward Robert Hughes (1851–1914), which is a watercolour and gouache on paper, painted in 1912 (bet he didn't know he only had two more years to live when he painted it). I had my head cocked to one side so I looked all refined and knowledgeable, when in fact all I'd done was read and memorise the little brass plaque. I was in fact deep in thought – thinking that it was a wonderfully inspiring picture depicting Night as a beautiful winged lady carrying a tiny sleeping baby and behind her, with a train of other babies following. The babies were the stars, or that's how I interpreted it.

Bless.

Will never look at a star in the same way again.

Anyway, was looking at this wonderful painting and wondering what it was supposed to represent – other than my superficial interpretation – when a deep voice spoke behind me.

'It's very inspiring isn't it? I like to think that Night is leading the stars away from daylight, so they don't get lost in the brightness of the sun. Night gives way to Day, and takes her children with her. What do you think?'

Crikey, hadn't thought of anything but that was pretty good. Decided that I would agree and put a far-away, whimsical look on my face in the hope of looking refined and clever. I turned around and found myself staring into the brightest blue eyes I had ever seen. They were partially hidden beneath a flop of sandy hair which the clever stranger had to keep pushing out of his eyes. He was rather good looking, and in any other circumstances I would have stayed and chatted, but I had to make sure I was available for my toy-boy, so I gave him the briefest of replies.

214

'I wasn't really able to think of anything, and thank goodness! I don't think I could come up with anything better than yours. That was lovely. Now bugger off. I'm waiting for a little boy to come and practise his chat-up lines on me, and if he wants, he can pay for sex later, for which I imagine I'll have to give him marks out of ten.' 'Cept I didn't say any of the last stuff, I just thought it in my head.

Was totally unprepared for his response.

'So far so good then?'

Eh?

He held out his hand to introduce himself. 'You must be Chloe?' he continued.

'Eh?'

Must have looked a bit thick standing there with a vacant look on my face and my mouth hanging open. Very attractive though.

He laughed and told me that he was Jason.

I mean Fred.

Yup. He was my date. And jolly nice he was too.

We toured the whole of the museum and he talked about the paintings with a passion that was contagious. He gave each one we looked at a life of its own. The subjects had lives and families and passions that I wouldn't have imagined; they were no longer just images caught on canvas, they were tangible, tragic, heroic people immortalised forever. I was captivated by each and every word. He was getting a ten out of ten so far.

Hurrah! No need for lies. Not yet anyway.

Finally we entered the Egyptian and Roman exhibition and I was in my element. There was a burial cave dated something BC that was full of skeletons and Roman tablets inscribed with the dates and names of departed loved ones, many of them slaves. I wanted to impress so I decided to impart some of my Roman history knowledge to Fred and

215

told him that if a slave wanted to be a free man – or woman – they had to wait for their master to place their name on the town's Roll of Citizens. Once their name appeared on the list the slave could then set themselves up in business. Without that, they could be free but would have no means of support, so would never truly be free.

Wasn't sure if I had remembered it right or not but it sounded damn good. And he was indeed impressed, at least I hoped the look on his face was a glazed look of impression. Could have been boredom, but who on earth can be bored in a room full of dead bodies?

I was on a roll. I think I talked him to death because when I looked up he was staring at me with a smile on his face.

Was very self-conscious at this point.

He was really staring.

Was worried that I might have dried bogey flapping in my nose, so I turned away and had a quick furtle.

Phew, nothing there.

Then I felt his hand on my shoulder and he turned me back round to look at him.

Crikey!

I was supposed to be out with a pale-skinned choirboy who'd never had a date before and who was so shy and unworldly that he had to pay someone to go out with him, and yet I was standing in front of a man who was totally in control, held the most enchanting conversations and who could hold my gaze with the most mesmerising stare. I was also certain that he was slightly older than twenty-four.

I was ashamed to realise that I had butterflies in my stomach. Eek.

Dangerous.

Mustn't form attachments to clients. They are the client. I am the whore. Above all, must never ever, *ever* believe in the Mills & Boon moment. The one where the dashing hero, who has just the right amount of bastard in him to be sexy,

216

scoops the weak and feeble heroine into his arms and tells he is going to kiss her, damn it, and she *will* enjoy it and he *will* take her away from all this and make her happy.

Must never ever believe in the above.

But crikey it was easy to get carried away.

He was still staring at me, *really* staring at me as though he wanted to see through me, beyond the surface and deep into the real Chloe. I had to look away from him. No one must see the real Chloe. Not even me.

'Why do you do this?' The question came completely out of the blue and I wasn't prepared, so I did what I was always did. I pretended that I had misunderstood the question and played dumb.

'Do what? Come to the museum? I don't, it was where you wanted to meet. Did you want to go somewhere else? We can. Anywhere you want. You're paying.' Am very good at gabbling and filling those annoying silences with inane chatter. But it didn't work this time. He placed his hand gently on my elbow and ushered me towards the door. 'You're not the same as the others. This isn't you. Come with me.'

He held my hand as we walked down the sweeping marble steps and it was the most intimate and electrifying gesture. I wanted to go home. I didn't want to do this, I didn't want to be paid to go on a date and have these forbidden feelings. I wanted to be free when I had these feelings again.

Felt like a Roman slave with big fat crush on her master.

I wanted to *know* that I was free, not only from what I was doing now, but from any ghostly emotions I might still be carrying.

I liked being able to switch off. I liked being in control. But I wasn't in control any longer, and I was afraid of where this would lead and what would happen afterwards and how I would cope.

But I let him hold my hand in his and I followed his lead

217

and it led straight to a café bar where he ordered hot chocolate and coffee cake.

Of all the things to order, he chose comfort food.

Perhaps he was an angel.

Perhaps he was my very own Clarence and I would find myself in Bedford Falls crashing cars and getting drunk, only to discover that life really is worth living, and it doesn't actually matter what situation you find yourself in, it's who's there with you, and who can help you get back on track again, that matters most.

Whatever he was, it was freaking me out and I was looking for the perfect opportunity to leave. Maybe this man got his rocks off by breaking women down, by burrowing into their lives and finding out what made them tick.

What made me tick?

Hot chocolate and coffee cake for one.

And Greg.

Greg used to make me tick like hell, though not in the same way. That was more in a stressed 'can't control this ticking and twitching' sort of way.

Fred was different. If indeed Fred was his name. He actually wanted to know *me*.

He seemed gentle and kind, and in touch with the emotional side of living. Perhaps he wasn't an angel, perhaps he was gay.

I found two seats by the smoked glass windows, great big comfy chairs with enough room to tuck your feet up underneath your bottom and with big fat arms wide enough to rest a cup of hot chocolate on. I watched as he waited for the order, and noticed that he was very methodical and precise. He paid and threw the change into a little pot on the counter, then paused and looked around the small, dimly-lit room until he saw me.

And he smiled at me.

And it felt like heaven. It was just the smallest of smiles and yet its effect was electrifying. I shivered and told myself to behave.

He was a client. A 'gentleman'.

He bought the cake and hot chocolate back to the table and sat opposite me.

Neither of us spoke.

I didn't look at him or touch my cake, I just sat staring at my hands, wondering what the hell was going on and not wanting to deal with the situation, while in the background Frank Sinatra told me that it had to be me.

You can only look at your hands for so long until they get boring and you have to look up again. When I did finally look up and smile at him, he did no more than reach across the table and take my hands in his. He held them and turned them over in his own rather larger, powerful but ever so nice hands, and he looked at me quizzically.

I looked back, and couldn't speak. Didn't think a croak would be very attractive and that would be all I could manage.

'What did you see?'

'Eh?' What the fuck was he talking about?

'What did you see in your hands? Did they answer your questions? Or are you still waiting for the answers to all your questions?'

Hell. He was a mind reader. He wasn't Jason at all. He was Uri Gellar. Only ever so slightly more pretty.

'Erm.' Great response! Well done Chloe! Where was the verbal diarrhoea when I needed it?

'You know only you have the answers, don't you? You just have to know what questions to ask yourself.'

Deep.

'What was the first thing you thought when Fiona called you and told you about me, Chloe?'

Erm, that I was about to break in an ugly pre-pubescent twat that looked like a Virginia Andrews character.

Decided it was best if I stayed silent.

'Did you want to meet me, or am I just a way of escaping? What are you running from?'

Who the fuck was this? I began to wonder if I was on some sick reality TV show and began to look round the room for tell-tale signs of cameras. Don't know what the tell-tale signs of cameras are so didn't do too well, but was on my guard. Also straightened my back and corrected my posture. What would mother think if she saw her prostitute daughter on TV with slouchy shoulders? 'No need to let yourself go just because you're a pro, dear', that's what.

He carried on, undeterred by my silence. 'What do you want to do? Right now, what would make you happy?'

'To be held, to know that I'm wanted, to know that I'm good enough for someone, to know that I'm *enough* for someone, to feel safe. To be able to trust again. To believe that things really will get better. To know that time is a great healer.'

Shit in hell! Where had that come from? Did I really say it out loud?

'How do you think you can start believing?'

Had indeed said it out loud.

'I don't know. I'm afraid to believe. I *won't* believe.'

He let go of my hands and looked at me. I turned my head away and stared out of the window, but I could still feel his eyes on me. I could also feel the first tears of pity welling in my eyes and fought to control them.

'I don't think I can ever believe again. I don't want to.'

'Why don't you want to believe, Chloe? We all believe in something. Isn't that what gets us through?'

'If you believe in things then you can be hurt. You'll end up disappointed and alone.' AHA! Now I had him, he didn't have all the answers.

'But surely you can also end up happy and fulfilled. If we don't have hopes and dreams then we won't follow them, and we'll never have anything to strive for. What makes you get out of bed every day? What are you working towards? What are your dreams, your ambitions?'

Shit. He was good. Really, really good. I hadn't looked at it like that. What *were* my dreams? Right now the only dream I had was to not let my tears escape from my dazzlingly wet eyes. I looked at him and plop! Out came a tear.

He didn't move and he didn't mention the tear, thank goodness.

'I just want to belong again. I want to feel as though I've come home. But I don't know where home is any more, or where I am, or where I'm going. I'm just drifting, and I have no control. I think that perhaps I don't deserve to belong.'

Another goddam self-pitying tear plopped out to join its friend. I waited for him to say something, but for a long time he just looked at me, until I had to look away again.

'Why don't you belong, Chloe? Why don't you *deserve* to belong?'

Okay, if he wanted it, he could have it!

'If I deserved to belong then I would. I wouldn't be here in this life, I'd be in my old one, with my husband, and my house and my job and my goddam fucking cats that I'll never see again. I used to belong! I used to have the fairytale! But I was thrown out of the castle and replaced with another princess so the fairytale ended and reality began! That's why I don't belong! *We* don't validate ourselves, *we* don't decide we belong, *others* do, and we just go along with it. So when you've been told you're not good enough, and you've been *shown* you're not good enough as many times as I have, you start believing it. That's why I won't ever believe again!'

My voice was all hissy and rather sexy or so I thought, and another tear plopped out onto my cheek, and soon there was river washing its way down my face, but I carried on, the

221

floodgates were open and it was my turn. It was finally my turn.

'And don't tell me I have no right to cry. Don't tell me I have no right to feel sorry for myself and don't you *dare* tell me that I'm in control of my own life, because if that was true I wouldn't be sitting here now talking to a man who has paid for my company. I'd be with someone who wants to be with me for who I am and not what they can buy from me. Don't you dare tell me that I have no right to feel angry! I have every right, and don't you dare sit there and judge me!'

I was right! I *didn't* have to be ashamed of feeling sorry for myself at all! It wasn't *all* my fault. It was *partly* my fault, but I didn't have to take all of the blame. I didn't ask Greg to go off and shag a slack-assed slut. I didn't make him marry me; it wasn't my fucking fault.

Phew! I felt a little better, but the tears still fell.

Fred handed me a hanky and reached across the table for my hand again. He held it gently in his, and asked me more questions.

'Tell me what happened to you. Tell me why you're here, why you do this?'

And so I did.

I told him everything.

And now I'm home, and I'm going to bed, and I'm never going to see Fred again, but I'll always be glad I met him. Perhaps this *was* my road.

Maybe my life has been taking its rightful path after all, maybe I am meant to be exactly where I am, and who I am; because without Fred I doubt that I would have exorcised my demons, and without choosing the path I did, I wouldn't have met Fred, and I certainly wouldn't have had the courage to explore and question the only person that can get me out of this. The only person that can save me.

Me.

Chloe Louise Elizabeth Richards.

## 9 January

I slept for almost twelve hours, and I didn't wake once: no dreams, no nightmares, just blissful peaceful sleep. And I feel refreshed and optimistic and I think I can finally start taking control again. Except this time I believe it when I say it, I'm not just paying lip-service.

Yay for handsome men who claim to be little boys wanting sexual advice.

I wonder who he really is?

I wonder why he chose me?

Think I'll call Fiona and ask her.

### 16.23

Fiona was useless. She only knows that he's very rich and can pay, and came with high praise. She also wanted to know why I was asking. 'You're not forming an attachment are you, darling? Not with a client. We know the rules don't we.'

We certainly did know the rules, and rules sucked.

But I wasn't going to, at least not any more.

So I quit.

Just like that.

Have told her that I don't want to work for her any more. Think I confused her a little because she offered me a pay rise.

'Whatever you've been offered, Chloe, I can match it and more. You're better off with me. I *know* you. They'll just palm you off onto anyone.'

'Fiona, I'm stopping. I don't want to do it any more. I never wanted to do it, I just fell into it. I'm sorry, do I owe you anything? Is there some sort of notice period I have to buy myself out of?'

She laughed at me.

Well I didn't know! I wasn't up on the etiquette of quitting a job as a hooker.

'No darling, just have fun, and remember that if everything else fails, at least you've got yourself to fall back on, and you can always cash in on that.'

Hmm, what a splendid thought.

I just said thank you and hung up.

And that's it. I'm unemployed! I'm blissfully without a job. I can do what I want and when I want, and I will.

It's all about to happen for me!

## 11 January

*08.15*

Hmm . . .

Have had call from Sophia.

'Darling, have you seen the glossies?'

'The what-ies?'

'Oh darling, it's Sunday, you know, the *glossies.*'

'Ah, in that case then, no, I don't have kids, I was in bed – sleeping, not reading.'

'Think you should get them. Very interesting. I'll call you later. Give my love to your mother when she calls.'

Eh?

And that was it – she rang off.

Why on earth would my mother call?

*08.30*

Shit. Hope I didn't invite mum for Sunday tea. Am sure I would remember.

*08.35*

Am not sure of the etiquette on buying Sunday papers. Am I allowed to go into paper shop looking as though I've just got out of bed? Will of course remove crusty bits from my eyes beforehand. Or should I wear a tracksuit and look as though I wasn't about to waste my Sunday morning snuggled up in bed but am in fact about to begin training for the London Marathon? In which case why would I be buying the Sunday papers? Surely one cannot run while having Sunday papers shoved under one's arm?

Perhaps I should dress as though I've just come from church. Or indeed am just about to go to church. Then again, I don't want to look sad – I don't want people to look at me and think 'she hasn't got anywhere to go on a Sunday. She hasn't got anyone to take her out for a nice walk or meal or country shag. She's a sad lonely cat keeper'.

Hmm.

Do I have to wear make-up? Never know who I might meet.

Bugger it.

Have to plan a 'Sunday paper buying' wardrobe.

*08.56*

Have decided on pyjamas, furry boots, big long coat and the finger in the eye to remove crusty bits look.

Hurrah!

Can now come back to flat, remove coat and climb back into bed with a big cup of coffee and perhaps sleep a bit more. Wonder why it's so important to buy the 'glossies' anyway?

Fugger!

What paper should I buy? Don't know which glossy Sophia was talking about.

*09.09*

Am silly. Of course I know what paper she buys. It has the

best Sunday glossies and the most fabulous outfits and within seconds of seeing the fabulous outfits, Sophia will have bought them. So am off to buy the *Sunday Sport*.
Or something similar.

Fuggering, buggering shitting hell!! Am moving. Am having face lift. Am about to be put up for adoption. Am splashed across pages of high-class glossy.

Sophia has called again, asking if I'd bought the glossies yet. Told her yes. Told her I went to supermarket looking like piece of shit. Told her as I walked into the supermarket looking like piece of shit I saw several people flicking through the Sunday glossies. One old man was looking rather sheepish as he flicked through a well-thumbed supplement and he cast me a furtive glance. Then he looked back at his glossy, had a furtle with something in his pocket, and then looked back at me. *Then* he had a furious furtle that lasted a quite a long time.
Eugh!
Thought perhaps he was reading a *Sunday Sport* supplement and being a dirty old man. Was about to tell him that there was a time and a place for things like that, and standing in the magazine section of Sainsbury's clearly wasn't one of them.
Then I stopped in my tracks.
It wasn't a *Sunday Sport* supplement at all. It was a nice, classy supplement. A nice, classy, high-gloss broadsheet supplement.
Had picture of a pretty woman on the front. She was wearing a very nice coat – in fact I had the same coat. Hurrah for me and my high-class fashions. She was also standing inside

226

a museum with her head cocked to one side looking very intellectual and refined and ever so slightly unapproachable. I studied the picture and saw that she was looking at *Night with her Train of Stars* by Edward Robert Hughes (1851–1914).

Hmm.

I had recently been to the museum and looked at *Night with her Train of Stars* by Edward Robert Hughes (1851–1941), and had worn same coat. Had also stood with head cocked to one side looking very intellectual and refined and ever so slightly unapproachable.

Hmm.

Was *me* on front page of nice glossy magazine – not how I imagined it to be when I was a little girl.

EUGH!

Was an old man standing in Sainsbury's, getting his rocks off over pictures of *me*.

EUGH!

Sophia tried to calm me down, but it didn't work.

'Oh darling, they've blanked out most of your face. No one will know.'

'They haven't blanked out my face at all, they've just put a black strip across my eyes. I look like a hostage.'

'No one will know it's you – stop worrying. Anyway, is it true?'

'Is what true?'

'What he says, is it true?'

'I haven't read it yet. I can't look. Shit, what about my mother?'

'Are you joking? This is your mother we're talking about, she'll love it. Her daughter is being paid three thousand pounds for sex. She always knew you were a cut above the rest. This'll be dinner fodder for years.'

She was probably right.

A coup is a coup, and this certainly outdid Marjorie Westerly's son being arrested for importing hard core porn and selling it on. And him being one of the youngest superintendents in the local force as well. Still, if police officers don't want to buy hard core porn then one can only assume that Christ does indeed walk among us once more.

Nope, mum would be pleasantly aghast.

Sophia has gone and I'm left staring at a picture of myself and wondering if I'll spend the rest of my life being duped by men.

Probably.

Am a fool.

Am far too trusting.

Stupid, stupid me.

Can now banish all thoughts of being rescued by a dashing young man called Fred.

Fred is a wanker.

*12.03*
Am going to become lesbian.

*12.15*
Don't do women though. Think I've said that several times in the past few months.

*12.23*
Might do women if I was drunk, just to see. I think all women are a little curious. I bet all women secretly wonder what it would be like to have sex with another woman, but a lot of women will deny it. Those women are liars. I wonder. I just don't think I'd do anything about it. Also, can't see myself settling down with a woman.

Nope, need someone with dangly bits.

Who isn't a wanker.

Darn it.

*12.32*
Am going to become a nun. Think a wimple will suit my colouring. Ooh, and can have an affair with a rather dashing priest. Am back onto the Richard Chamberlain thing again.

*12.55*
Have got to read article. Is it wrong to open a bottle of tequila at one o'clock on the Lord's Day?
Nope.

*14.00*
Hmm.

*14.37*
Am crying big fat 'sorry for me' tears. Was actually a rather moving article and if it hadn't been about me I would be having rather squishy thoughts about the man who could write such a touchingly accurate piece of poetry. A man called Frederick Mills.
Am also rather pleased with the photographs. There is one rather tragic picture of me staring out of the window of the café bar, it's rather blurry and I'm barely recognisable, but I look forlorn and far away, and the caption beneath reads: 'When the dreaming ends and reality bites'. Think it's a rather clever caption and very true.
Don't do dreams.
What's the point?
They only end in tears.
Good things never last.
Deal with the here and now and never, ever dream.

It is clear that Fred manipulated me from start to finish. He must have had the photographer follow me into the museum and take several shots of me before he arrived; they had probably prearranged the café and the photographer had no doubt set up outside before Fred and I arrived.

I had been far too trusting. Had harboured romantic Mills & Boon thoughts about Fred as well. Silly thoughts that little girls have. Stupid little girls that don't know any better and haven't had their dreams torn from them. I allowed myself to glimpse a better place; a place where hope still exists and people can trust without feeling foolish or vulnerable.

Am silly.

Am going to sleep.

Will feel better when I wake up.

### 19.00

Crikey, have been asleep for a rather long time. Keep hearing ringing and then it stops, must have dreamt it.

### 19.07

Am very worried about me. Can still hear ringing, it's very distant, and I don't know where it's coming from.

### 19.22

It's coming from my knicker drawer! My knickers shouldn't be ringing. I don't use the knicker phone any more. I'm no longer in 'business'.

Will ignore my knickers.

### 19.40

Am trying to watch *Coronation Street* but my knickers are very persistent. Will have to answer them, or at least turn them off.

### 19.53

Have missed eight knicker calls – all from the same number, have no idea who it is.

Am not going to call them back, I'm not in business – probably a wrong number anyway.

*20.17*
Uh-oh! There go my French frillies. I'm totally pissed off now so will answer them.

*21.03*
What a bizarre day this is turning out to be. Was my journalist friend Fred. Or rather that lying shit Fred. Appears he wants to meet me 'to explain'. Told him to bugger off and then put the phone down. He called back and asked me to please not put the phone down again.
So I put the phone down again.
Persistent little bugger called back so I told him my soul wasn't for sale and put the phone down again.
Why on earth would I want to meet him? Perhaps he wants to buy the film rights to my life story.
Horrid man.

*22.35*
Have had very long afternoon nap and yet am still very sleepy, don't know what's wrong with me. Can't get enough sleep.
Thank God this day is over.

*22.45*
Am very scared. My knickers are ringing again and some-one's at my front door.
Will ignore both.
Have *got* to answer door. The neighbours will complain if I don't. Wish I had a little spyhole thing, will have to shout through letter box instead like old spinster-type person. Will have to hope that the person on the other side of the door is honest. So, if they answer 'An axe-wielding maniac,' to my 'Who is it?' question, I'll know not to answer.

*04.30*
Was not an axe-wielding maniac.
Was Fred.


## 22 January

Is it better to have loved and lost, than never to have loved
at all?
No.
It is better to have loved and lost, and *know* that you were
also loved, once.
I *was* loved.
Once.
And I will be again.


## 25 January

Hmm.
Fred is such a lovely name.
Hmm.
Fred.
Freeeed.
Freddy.
Freddy Weddy.
Uh-oh.
Am going off on one again.
But it doesn't matter.
I'm allowed.
Am allowed to do and think anything I want.
The world, it appears, is my oyster.
And this oyster contains a pearl . . .

And that's where my diary ends.

There is no happy ending, because there *is* no ending, it's still being written; but life will get better and time really is a great healer.

I will never again believe in the everlasting, because the everlasting belongs to childhood dreams. Most little girls are bought up believing in the fairytale: one day their prince will come, and somewhere over the rainbow dreams really do come true. But then little girls grow up, and they realise that perhaps they don't need a prince after all, they just need someone to share their journey, and that somewhere, through the storm clouds, and over the rainbow, dreams may not always come true, but there is a little pot.

And it is full of hope.

Always hope.

And that's where I am now.

I have weathered the stormclouds and climbed the rainbow, and I realise that though fairytales may not come true, there is a future.

It's just that my future lies beyond the yellow brick road. And one day I will once again be Home.

**The End . . .**

. . . except for this bit:

That fateful night in December, when my husband of six months stayed out all night, he told me that he did nothing more than take part in a philosophical discussion.

The topic up for debate was: 'Should someone be punished for their actions, or for the consequences of their actions?'

Ooh the irony . . .

Now that really is:

The End